EVIL FTW!

Volume Two

Art and Story by
Sara "Selan" Pike

Evil FTW Volume Two
Book 2 of the Evil FTW Series

Published by Epicycle Studios llc.

Websites:
http://epicyclestudios.com
http://evilftw.tumblr.com

Volume Two

Episodes 31-70

Art and Story by Sara "Selan" Pike

Originally published on
http://evilftw.tumblr.com

Welcome back to Evil FTW (that's still For the Win)! I'm glad you've stayed with me so far.

In this volume, the story really begins to hit its stride. We flesh out the supporting cast more, and meet our main antagonist.

I do want to spend a little time talking about episode 31, however. When an artist or writer looks back at anything they've made something like ten years ago, there's always going to be a certain level of cringe involved. This is especially exacerbated when the author is, as I am, a queer individual, looking back at things they've written about gender and sexuality that reflect old, toxic viewpoints that they had once internalized.

What I'm saying is, episode 31 has problems and it bothers me.

Something I tell people about EvilFTW is that since I started it before I came out of the closet, it starts off very straight and becomes gayer over time. That's true. But it also means that parts of these early stories offend me at times!

I contemplated changing the content of that chapter for this compilation. I agonized for a long time over how I could improve it with the fewest amount of changes. Instead, I decided to leave it as it is, because changing it now won't change how the me back in the early 2000's felt. I had a lot of bad assumptions in my head regarding gender, and those ideas actively prevented me from understanding my own gender identity until much later in my life.

I was still learning, back then. I'm still learning now.

Thank you for your understanding.

(It's a Saturday! Selan is out looking at hair clips, wondering how exactly they work. At some point, a girly-looking person glances over, trying to see the shelf Selan's standing in front of. Selan moves out of the way.)

Selan:
Excuse me. ^^;;

Girly person:
Thanks. ^^ **(Person reaches over and grabs a pair of hair clips.)**

Selan:
Holy craps, man! =O Where did you get that dress?

Person:
I made it. With my girlfriend.

Selan:
Aww I'm jealous. I can't sew anything =<

Person:
I could try to teach you if you'd like. But I'm not so good myself n_n; She's teaching me.

Selan:

I dunno, I've tried to learn… it's the measuring things that gets me. **(She tugs at her sleeve.)** I always make one sleeve bigger than the other.

Person:

Oh, I can't make the seams straight. **(Little laugh, pause…)** You know I'm a boy, right?

Selan:

Yeah. You've got like, **(she motions at her face)** masculine features. Kinda?

Person (smiling):

I'm Kesava, by the way. >_>; Oh and, I'm not gay. Not that that's wrong, but…

Selan:

Well yeah, you said you had a girlfriend.

Kesava:

Most people think that's a metaphor.

Selan:

Nuh uh, cuz if you were gay you'd probably be the girl in the… er… ^^;;

Kesava (laughing):

You're funny.

Selan:

^^;; Heh…

Kesava:

I'm sorry if I'm hard to understand. I don't speak English so good.

Selan:

You kidding? You should hear this other friend of mine! He's got this real thick accent… if not for me he'd still be all like, "Listen to me! I do not know what word 'the' is meaning!"

Kesava:

Sounds like a friend of mine.

Selan:

Yeah? What's your friend's name?

Kesava:

Selanio. He's from Russia.

Selan:

Ah! Oh emm gee!!

Kesava:

What?

Selan:

My friend's Selanio!

Kesava:

Oh my. Coincidence, I suppose.

Selan:

Yeah. Aww man. That's funny, I always assumed Selanio didn't have any friends.

Kesava:

Really? We've known each other since we were little boys.

Selan:

Huh. **(She pauses, thinking.)** I can't imagine Selanio as a little boy. I'm pretty sure he just congealed somewhere, full-grown, moustache and all.

Kesava:

The moustache was odd >_> He said it would make him look more villainous.

Selan:

It does, I guess… makes him look kinda creepy, that's for sure. But after all this time, I think he'd look weird without it ^^;

Kesava:

I don't suppose you know how I could get a hold of Selanio, do you? I've been needing to speak with him.

Selan:

Hey, no problem! I live with him, see.

Kesava:
Really? He never told me that.

Selan:
Whaaaaat! =< Did he even mention me at all?

Kesava:
Well, he mentioned some "weird girl" he lived with… and something about Mudkips, whatever that is.

Selan:
;o; "Weird girl"?! … and what is that loser's problem with Mudkips, that's what I want to know… >_>

Kesava:
What's a Mudkip?

Selan:
It's a pokeyman. You know, like, let me show you my… er…

Kesava:
What?

Selan:
Nevermind. -_-; Let's go see Selanio.

(A little later, Selan and Kesava are walking into the house.)

Selan (closing the door behind them):
Selaaaaanio! There's someone here to see you!

Selanio (yelling from his bedroom):
Who is it?

Selan:
Guess!

Selanio:
Is it a hot chick?

Selan:
Totally!

(Selanio walks out of his room.)

Selanio:
Hey, that's not a hot chick, that's a Kesava.

Kesava:
^^;;

Selan:
Hey, *I'm* a hot chick.

Selanio:
Hah! You keep telling yourself that. u_u

Selan:
You're so mean! TT-TT

Selanio (ignoring Selan):
Man, Kesava, I haven't seen you in ages!

Kesava:
Not since we started college. n_n

Selanio:
What brings you to town, man?

Kesava:
It's my spring break right now.

Selanio:
Jeez, this early?

Kesava:
Yes.

Selan:
Selan is ignored. TToTT

Selanio:
Why don't you go out and get some food or something?

Selan:
What, food for you?

Selanio:
Yes.

Selan:
Why should I? =O

Selanio:
Because you're hungry too so you might as well.

Selan:
Am not.

Selanio:
That's a lie. You're *always* hungry.

Selan:
Damn…

Selanio (throwing his wallet at her):
Get Selanio a burger, woman. u_u

Selan:
Jeez! =<

Kesava (sitting on the couch):
Selanio… =(

Selanio:
Whaaat?

Selan:
I'm stealing all the money in your wallet.

Selanio:
You better not!

Selan:
I'm doin' it! I'm doin' it!!

(She leaves)

Selanio:
Ugh. **(He sits down.)** See what I have to deal with?

Kesava:
^^;

Selanio:
So… man! It's so good to see you.

(Xeno wanders out of his room. He spots the newcomer, and walks into the living room.)

Xeno:
Hey, Selanio. Who's your friend?

Selanio:
This is Kesava.

Xeno (smoothing out his hair):
Does Kesava have a boyfriend…?

Kesava:
I have a girlfriend.

Selanio:
Kesava's a man, man.

Xeno:
Oh, ha ha. -_O

Selanio:
I'm serious!

Kesava:
It's true.

Selanio:
He's got a PENIS.

Xeno:
o_o; Urk…

Selanio:
Hah!! Xeno was gonna put the moves on you!

Kesava:
It happens… n_n;; >_> More than I'd like it to…

Xeno:
>_< Jeez…

Selanio:
High five!

(Kesava unenthusiastically high-fives Selanio.)

Kesava:
But anyway…

Selanio:
Hm?

Kesava:
I actually came by for a reason.

Selanio:
What's that? Got any people you need me to blow up?

Kesava:
No, no… I just wanted to give you a heads up. From what I hear, Stesha Zitomira's moving back to this area.

Selanio:
Whaaat? No, can't be. He's going to… to that school near where his dad lives.

Kesava:
That's just it. His father got a job here, so Stesha came with him. He's transferring to your school.

Selanio:
What?! But—but he can't transfer in the middle of the term!

Kesava:
Sure he can. -_-; His father's rich, remember. All he has to do is donate a nice healthy sum to the school and he can do anything he wants.

Selanio:
Goddammit!

Xeno:
Wait. So who's this Stesha guy?

Selanio:
The bane of my existence. -_O

Kesava:
He's an old friend of ours from high school. n_n; And by friend, I mean…

Selanio:
You mean a son of a bitch who annoyed the hell of me day in and day out and ratted out all my schemes and tried to sabotage every relationship I got into. >_<

Xeno:
Jeez. Think you can just avoid him?

Selanio:
I doubt it. -_-; He seeks me out. It's like he's got Selanio-seeking radar on him.

Kesava:
Yeah. =\ I don't know why, but he's really got it out for you…

Selanio:
He's just jealous because I'm such a sexy bitch.

Xeno:
snerk… heh… heheheh…

Selanio:
What's so funny? >_O

Xeno:
You… a sexy bitch… hahahah!

Selanio (punching Xeno in the arm):
Shut up, ugly. -_O

(Meanwhile! Selan is at a nearby burger joint, feeling pretty miffed. She waits in line, mumbling to herself.)

Selan:
Stupid Selanio… I'm gonna have them put extra mustard on that burger. Fucker hates mustard. >_< That'll show 'im..

(Someone behind her taps her on the shoulder. She jolts and turns around.)

Selan:
What, what?!

Person who's smiling a little too much:
I was just wondering if you knew what time it was?

Selan:
Oh. **(She gets out her cell phone and looks at it)** It's five thirty.

Person:
Thank you. n_n I'm Stesha, by the way.

(Dun dun dunnnnnn!!)

Selan:
What was that noise?

Stesha:
Intercom malfunction, maybe? What's your name?

Selan:
Okay. I'm Selan. Nice eye.

Stesha:
Er… thanks.

-End: Episode thirty-one.

(It's 5 o'clock on a Saturday, about a week since last we saw our villains. Selan is at the house, toying with the stereo system.)

Selan (to herself):

Xeno's workin' late… Selanio's out with some chick… Selan's got the house to herself and it's *party time!*

(Selan cranks up the volume and the room is filled with the sound of obnoxiously cheery music. She starts dancing.)

Selan:

Woooo!

(Selan goes on like this for a while, alternating playing around on the computer in her room and dancing like a moron in the living room. At around 5:30, the door opens and Selanio walks in, followed by his date: a pretty blonde girl with a perfect figure and big boobs. Selan is dancing around.)

Selan (obliviously singing):

Not to put too fine a point on it, say I'm the only bee in your bonnet, make a little birdhouse in your— heh?

Selanio?

Selanio:
No, don't stop, this is hilarious.

Selan (turning off the stereo):
What the crap are you doing here? Don't you two have dinner reservations or something?

Selanio:
Selanio forgot his wallet. Can't get dinner without a wallet.

Selan:
Oh. Uh. Go get it, then.

Selanio:
I intend to. u_u **(to his date)** Anya, you can go sit on the couch.

Anya:
'Kay.

(Anya sits on the couch while Selanio goes to his room. Selan awkwardly sits on the other couch, scratching her head.)

Selan:
Sooo. Ti studyentka?

Anya:
Huh?

Selan:
That was Russian. Cuz, yanno, Selanio's Russian. You a student?

Anya:
Oh. Yeah. I'm a sophomore.

Selan:
Hmmm. Selan too. What's your major?

Anya:
Well, it was biology, but now I'm thinking of switching to film.

Selan (losing interest):
Huh. Interesna. =d

Selanio (walking back in):
Okay Selan, stop scaring her.

Selan:
I am not! =O I'm making conversation.

Selanio:
Conversation with you is pretty scary for normal people. u_u

Selan:
What, so I'm abnormal?

Selanio:
That's right. Come on, Anya, let's get some food.

Anya (getting up):
Okay. **(To Selan)** It was nice meeting you.

Selan:
Good times, good times.

(Selanio and Anya leave. Selan grumbles as she walks back to the stereo.)

Selan:
Interrupting my awesome party. Stupid Selanio and that… that set of boobs on legs.

(She reaches over to the volume dial, pauses, and looks down at her own chest. She frowns, her face turning red.)

Selan:
I bet they're fake anyway! =O

(She turns the music on and wanders back to her room to use her computer.)

(About two hours later, Xeno comes home. Frowning at the annoying Japanese music Selan's playing, he turns off the stereo and pokes his head in Selan's room.)

Xeno:
You're gonna rot your mind with that stuff.

Selan:
Demo, kawaii desu yo~

Xeno:
It's stupid.

Selan:
Iie! Urusai!

Xeno:
-_-;; English?

Selan:
Shut uuuuup =<

Xeno:
Whatever…

(Xeno starts to leave)

Selan:
… uh… hey, Xeno?

(Xeno returns to Selan's door.)

Xeno:
What?

Selan (looking away, embarrassed):
Ano… Do you think my boobs are too small?

Xeno:
Where's this coming from?

Selan:
Well, I saw Selanio's date and she was all… va-VOOM. Yanno?

Xeno:
Seriously? Goddammit, why does Selanio get all the hot chicks…?

Selan:
Keep to the topic at hand please'kaythanks =<

Xeno:
Are you jealous of Selanio or something?

Selan:
Ew, no.

Xeno:
Oh, good. -_-; I don't think I need that sort of weirdness in my life…

Selan:
But seriously! I'm so small. =< I feel ugly.

Xeno:
You're not ugly. -_-

Selan:
But…

Xeno:
You look fine, Selan. You've got no reason to be self-conscious.

Selan:
Okay…

(Xeno leaves, going to his room. Selan sits at her computer for a little while more, drumming her fingers on the desk, until not long after when she hears Selanio coming in the front door. She hesitates, then walks out.)

Selan:
Hey.

Selanio:
Hey, loser. u_u

Selan:
=O Jerkface! u_u How'd the date go?

Selanio (plopping down onto the couch):
Eh, it was okay.

Selan:
Just okay?

Selanio:
Boring. This girl, she just talked and talked, all about herself.

Selan (sitting on the couch with him):
Selan can see why that would bother you. You get irritable when the conversation is not all about you.

Selanio:
Well, I am awesome. One could spend years talking about me. You see this? This thing we're doing? We're talking about me. Isn't it glorious?

Selan:
Sure. 9_9; So. No second date?

Selanio:
Gods no. >_<

Selan:
You sure? I mean, she was really pretty.

Selanio:
She wasn't *that* great-looking.

Selan:
You kidding? She had the… **(she makes little curvy motions with her hand)** She was practically a model.

Selanio:
She was topheavy. I think those boobs were fake.

Selan:
… =O THAT'S WHAT I SAID.

Selanio:
What?

Selan:
Nuffin' 6_6; **(She pauses.)** … Selanio, you don't think my boobs are too small, do you?

Selanio:
The hell kind of question is that?

Selan:
Selan was just wondering lately… you know.

Selanio:
Ah. Selanio sees. PMS. u_u You've become all weepy and girly.

Selan:

Shut up! =O

Selanio:

Selanio will humor your hormones, lest you become some horrible PMS-monster.

Selan:

TToTT I will kiiiillll you.

Selanio:

See? Nu, Selan's chest is fine. Selanio has always been of the opinion that as long as you've got enough for a handful you're good.

Selan:

Really?

Selanio:

Yep. And see, there's a test. **(He reaches over and grabs one of Selan's boobs.)** Yeah, these are fine. Not too small.

Selan (turning bright red):

You jerk!! **(She pulls away, then grabs a nearby pillow and starts pummeling him.)** Jerk! You can't do that!

Selanio:

Ow! Selanio was only answering your question!

Selan (still pummeling):

Selan's boobies are not for grabbing!

Selanio:

I was testing their size! I didn't want to, you asked!!

Selan (hitting harder):

You don't have booby-grabbing privileges!!! >_<

Selanio:

>_< Jeeeez! Stop it!

-End: Episode thirty-two.

Selanio:

Xeno, help! I've angered the PMS monster!!

(It's the afternoon. Selan is walking along the campus with Tavvy, who is trailing slightly behind her.)

Selan:
And then I was like… er… Tavvy?

Tavvy:
Hn?

Selan:
You look like you've been infected by the T-virus or something.

Tavvy:
I'm not a zombie.

Selan:
Not *yet*. You okay?

Tavvy:
Yeah. Yeah. I'm just… really tired. -_-;

Selan:
Did you get enough sleep last night?

Tavvy:
No. And I've been so busy lately…

Selan:
Busy with what?

Tavvy:
My job. Classes. Everything.

Selan:
Aw, I'm sorry.

Tavvy:
It's okay…

Selan:
But you seriously look sick. You think you've come down with something?

Tavvy:
I don't think so…

Selan:
Cuz if you're sick, stay away from me. My immune system sucks ass.

Tavvy: I'm really not…

(Tavvy proceeds to fall over, dropping his backpack.)

Selan:
Uh… shit! Tavvy, you okay?

Tavvy:
Uhn…

Selan:
Should I call a doctor?

Tavvy:
C-could you… get Professor Marika?

Selan:
He's not a doctor. =O Scary guys are not good for making you feel better!

Tavvy (getting his phone out and handing it to Selan):
I'm serious. Call him.

Selan:

You are a crazy person. =< **(She takes the phone, finds the Professor's number, and calls. She waits for the Professor to pick up, and…)** Ah, no. Tavvy's sick and he told me to call you and – umm… outside the physics building? - The front side. The one with the bike racks. - … okay? Bye.

(She hangs up and gives the phone back to Tavvy.)

Selan:

Seriously, you should see a doctor, not your scary boss. =<

Tavvy:

I'll be fine. **(He reaches for his bag, but can't seem to lift it off the ground. He drags it over instead.)** Weird…

Selan (taking the bag):

I'll carry it for—holy hell, this is heavy >_< No wonder you can't lift it.

Tavvy:

=<…

(Professor Marika walks up.)

Selan:

Well that was fast.

Marika:

I was nearby. **(To Tavvy)** What's wrong with you?

Tavvy:

I'm *sick.*

Marika (kneeling over, speaking very quietly so Selan can't hear):

You don't *get* sick.

Tavvy:

I know. I can't even lift my bag.

Marika:

Hm. **(He stands back up, takes Tavvy's bag from Selan, and puts it on over his shoulder. He then lifts Tavvy up.)** I'll take him to the doctor. You, run along.

Selan:

The infirmary is scary! Tavvy needs someone with him.

Marika:

Yes, and *I'll* be with him. Go away.

Tavvy:

It's okay, Selan. ^^;

Selan:

You sure?

Tavvy:

Yeah.

Selan:

Call me later, arrite?

Tavvy:

I will.

Selan:

And don't trust any doctor when they say something won't hurt!!

Tavvy:

O_o Okay.

Selan:

Bye~ **(Selan walks off.)**

Marika:

-_-; Well, she's annoying. That isn't the one you like, is it?

Tavvy:

What? What's wrong with her?

Marika:

9_9 Never mind. **(He starts carrying Tavvy down the road.)** So seriously, what's wrong with you?

Tavvy:

I don't know. >_< I'm tired and I've got this horrible pain in my stomach and I can't lift anything…

Marika:

That's worrying.

Tavvy:
I've never been sick since I got my powers. I was pretty sure I was immune to everything…

Marika:
You should be. You're about as resilient as I am, and I've never been sick a day of my life.

(They get to the English building and walk in.)

Tavvy:
So we're *not* going to the infirmary?

Marika:
I don't trust doctors. Especially considering, well… you.

Tavvy:
Right…

(They get to Marika's office and go in. Marika looks around for a suitable place to put Tavvy, but ends up laying him on the floor, for lack of a bed. Marika kneels next to Tavvy.)

Marika:
How long has this been going on?

Tavvy:
I don't know… I mean, I've been overworked so I thought I was just tired from that… the stomachache and weakness started just now. I fell over and everything.

Marika:
Hum. Perhaps something's gone wrong with your powers.

Tavvy:
I'm not losing them, am I?

Marika:
I wouldn't know. It would seem you've already acted out the purpose that Indrid guy had in mind for you, so…

Tavvy:
But I still have to save the world from a bunch of other stuff! Omen hasn't lost his powers, so I shouldn't lose mine, right?!

Marika:
Omen's powers probably aren't as demanding on his body as yours are.

Tavvy:
This isn't fair! >_<

Marika:
Don't go whining like that yet. We don't know what's going on.

Tavvy:
I need to talk to Indrid!

Marika:
That's all well and good, but we don't know how to contact him—short of knocking on the door of his moon base, but we haven't really got a rocket handy.

Tavvy:
Omen should know how to contact him! **(He starts to get up, but flinches and doubles over, clutching his stomach.)** Agh…

Marika:
Lay down. We don't know how to contact Omen either.

(Tavvy lays back down, still clutching his stomach.)

Tavvy:
Hnn… can I have any ibuprofen or something?

Marika:
I'm not sure how much good it'd do.

Tavvy:
Please?

Marika (sighing):
I'll run down to the 7-11 and get some…

Tavvy:
Thanks…

(Marika leaves the office, locking the door behind him so no one can bother Tavvy while's he's gone. He runs off campus to the nearest convenience store, then runs back. He walks back into his office to find that Tavvy's watch is beeping.)

Marika:
Are you going to check that? … Tavarius?

(Marika nudges Tavvy, but he doesn't respond. He kneels over and checks Tavvy's vitals—he's just unconscious, but his pulse is a little too fast. He frowns.)

Marika:
Shit. **(He looks at Tavvy's watch—it says that Ira's group is attacking.)** -_-; Perfect timing.

(Marika drops the bottle of ibuprofen on the floor near Tavvy and leaves, once again locking the door behind him.)

(Not much later, Lady Ira, Baron von Boom and Omen are causing trouble in town—throwing bombs, knocking over cars, overall just causing trouble… although, really, the Baron's the one doing most of the destruction.)

Omen:
So what's the point of this all, again?

Baron von Boom:
Having fun!

Lady Ira:
Blowing off steam. ^^; The Baron had a bad day, so…

Omen:
Hasn't he ever tried yoga or screaming into a pillow or something?

Baron von Boom (hurling a car into a nearby storefront):
We're supervillains! This is how we handle stress!

Omen:
If you say so… **(He uses his powers to fling a hot dog stand into a car.)**

Lady Ira:
Ira feels left out. Hey, Baron! Hand over some bombs!

Baron von Boom:
No! Mine! u_u

Lady Ira:
You jerk, stop hogging them!

Professor Pain (coming out of nowhere and tapping them on the shoulder):
Ahem.

Lady Ira:
Eep!!

Baron von Boom:
The hell? -_O Where's Apogee?

Professor Pain:
He's preoccupied at the moment. I need to speak with Omen. Where is… ah, there he is.

Baron von Boom (charging up an energy bolt):
Hey, wait, you— **(The Professor dashes, at super-speed, over to Omen. The Baron frowns.)** What the fuck…

Professor Pain (grabbing Omen by his scarf):
I need to contact Indrid.

Omen:
So what're you talking to *me* for?

Professor Pain:
He's *your* buddy, you ought to know how to get in touch with him.

Omen:
I don't have a clue where he is. I never contact him, he only contacts *me*.

Professor Pain (frowning, lifting Omen off the ground and shoving him into a wall):
Listen to me, it's imperative that Apogee speaks with Indrid!

Omen:
Indrid only appears when he's needed! If it's so damn 'imperative', then Indrid'll show up on his own.

Professor Pain:
Hmm. **(He pauses, dodges an energy bolt that the Baron throws at him, and counters by throwing Omen at the Baron.)** I'd recommend that the three of you go home. I'm feeling rather lenient today, so I think I can allow you to do that.

Baron von Boom (pushing Omen aside and standing back up):
Fuck you!

Lady Ira (nudging the Baron and whispering):
We can't fight him, yo. He's too powerful. Let's just go home and play Smash Brothers or something.

Baron von Boom:
But—

Omen (rubbing his neck, sore):
I'm on Ira's side. Let's get the hell out of here.

Baron von Boom:
>_<; You two suck.

Lady Ira (to the Professor):
Okay, we'll go home! But BE WARNED, OKAY! We'll have our vengeance!

Professor Pain (unimpressed):
I'm sure.

(Lady Ira, with some mock-drama, throws down a smoke bomb and the three villains escape. Professor Pain, meanwhile, runs back to the campus.)

(Marika arrives at the door to his office. He gets out his key-card to open the door, but stops when he hears voices coming from inside.)

Tavvy:
… it just doesn't seem fair. I get stuck with powers like this and hurt myself and have to deal with all this, and Omen… he gets to do whatever the hell he wants.

Indrid:
He has his own problems.

Tavvy:
Like what?

Indrid:
If he were to lose control of his emotions, his powers would go out of control. He must concentrate deeply at all times. It is difficult for him.

Tavvy:

Oh. **(Long pause.)** So if he had sex, would things just start flying around—

Indrid:

Do your kind always have to ask things like that?

Tavvy:

Sorry. **(He pauses again.)** Omen isn't really evil, though, is he?

Indrid:

No. He is not.

Tavvy:

I just don't get why he does this whole villain thing. I mean, I know you told him to, but he can quit now and he won't. Why would anyone want to be a villain if they aren't evil?

Indrid:

Very few people are truly evil, Mister Imogene. The world is more complicated than that.

Tavvy:

Yeah, maybe. **(He sighs.)** I'm kind of jealous, actually. They look like they have a lot of fun. For me, this hero-ing thing is all work, but for them it's more a game than anything.

Indrid:

Would you rather be a villain?

Tavvy:

… no. I don't think I could do it. I don't think I could even stand to just… I dunno, be neither. But still.

Indrid:

I am no longer in need of your powers, so it does not matter to me whether you continue to be a hero. Do you really wish to continue?

Tavvy:

… yeah. Yeah. I mean… the city needs me. The *world* needs me, I think. **(He chuckles.)** It's not like the Professor will do much of anything anymore.

(The Professor chooses this moment to unlock the door and

walk in.)

Marika:
Excuse me, what was that? -_O

Tavvy:
Ah! Professor! Er—I was just saying—ah—

Marika:
-_- Save it. **(To Indrid.)** What was wrong with him?

Indrid:
His body was rejecting his powers. I had feared that such a thing might happen at some point.

Marika:
Will he be okay?

Indrid:
Yes. I injected him with some medicine. I may have to do so again, but not for a few years.

Tavvy (going pale):
Wait, you… you put a *needle* in me?

Indrid:
Yes.

Marika:
He's terrified of needles, you know.

Indrid:
Which is why I did not wait for him to wake up before I injected him.

Marika:
Good thing.

Tavvy:
=<

Indrid:
I shall be going now.

Marika:
I assume you're not going to give us any number or anything we can call you at.

Indrid:
You assume correctly.

Marika:
Jeez…

Indrid:
I will see you in time. **(He leaves, closing the door behind him.)**

Marika:
So, what was it you were saying about me? -_O

Tavvy:
O_o Urk… uh… ^^;;; I think I'll just go on patrol, yeah? I think that's a good idea…

Marika:
Go on, then.

Tavvy:
n_n;;; Right…

(Tavvy runs off. Marika sighs, somewhat relieved, and sits at his desk.)

-End: Episode thirty-three.

034. You're so embarrassing.

(It's a weekend and we find our villains… at a wedding?! That's right. Selan, Xeno and Selanio have been invited to the wedding of Damon Lords and Dorcia Kamaria, and despite Selanio's protests they are in attendance. They're at the reception now, all dressed up fancy and eating food.)

Selan:
This is the most amazing thing I've ever seen.

Selanio:
It's just cake.

Selan:
It's ICE-CREAM cake. It's an ice-cream *wedding* cake. It's so amazing I can't even describe it! Oh gods, it's even got those crunchy bits in it!

Xeno:
Are you even allowed to eat that? Won't it kill you or something?

Selan:
It will not, shut up!

Selanio (resting his head on his hands, irritated):
Why are we even here? We don't even like these people.

Xeno:
Because we really didn't have anything better to do.

Selan:
Look, it's polite, you know? You can't just get invited to a wedding and not go.

Selanio:
Not going would probably be more polite than playing Kirby during the ceremony.

Selan:
But—but that preacher just wouldn't shut *up!* Besides, I've been wanting an excuse to wear this dress. You know, I bought it and this is the first time I've worn it. We never do anything fancy.

Selanio:
Why the hell would we do anything fancy?

Selan (shrugging):
Because we can? And you two look so cute in your suits! =D I swear I could just hug you both to death.

Selanio:
That's only because you've got a secret suit-and-tie fetish. -_-;

Selan:
I do not! =O

Xeno:
I'd hardly call it secret.

Selan:
Shut up!

(Clovis walks over and sits down.)

Clovis:
If she's got a suit fetish, I dare not imagine how she sees me.

Selan:
You guys suck and I hate you all. =<

Selanio:

What do *you* want? -_O

Clovis:

I'm bored as hell.

Xeno:

Welcome to the club.

(Selanio grins and steals Selan's purse.)

Selan:

Hey! What're you doing with that?!

Selanio:

Something awesome! Ah!

(He pulls out a marker and tosses the purse back at Selan. He takes the paper card that has the table number on it, and on the blank side of it writes "BOREDOM CLUB" on it. He leans the card against the centerpiece for all to see.)

Selan:

You're so embarrassing. =<

Xeno:

-_-;; I'm just going to ignore you and try to make conversation. So, Clovis.

Clovis:

Hm?

Xeno:

What're you doing these days, anyway? Didn't you say you had a new job, last time we saw you?

Clovis:

Yeah.

Xeno:

Care to elaborate…?

Clovis:

Not really, no.

Xeno:

Jeez…

Selanio:
He's trying to be mysterious, see. With his Armani suit and his emo hair and his "I won't tell you shit"!

Clovis:
Shut the fuck up, Yakov.

Selanio:
Godsdammit, why does everyone make Smirnoff jokes at me?

Xeno:
Because you ask for it?

Selanio:
He's Ukrainian! I'm Russian!

Clovis:
Like anyone knows the difference.

Selanio:
Ignorant sons of bitches! >_<

Selan (patting Selanio on the back):
It's okay, Selanio. I know the difference.

Selanio:
You do not. -_O

(Damon walks up and pulls up a chair. He smiles nervously.)

Damon:
May I join the boredom club?

Selanio:
No.

Selan:
^^;; Yes, yes.

(Damon sits down.)

Clovis:
Why so bored? It's *your* wedding, man.

Damon:
I hate long ceremonies like this. -_-; It's such a bother.

Selan:
Lemmie guess. Dorcia wanted the fancy wedding?

(Clovis laughs. He knows better.)

Damon:
No. n_n;; She hates these things more than I do. It's just that when the press watches you as much as they do me, you must do these things, lest the tabloids start to talk…

Selanio:
Well that's bunk.

Damon:
I know. -_-;

Selanio:
And damn but this reception is long. Selanio doesn't understand why, everyone knows that the people being married are in more of a hurry to leave. -_-;

Selan:
Why's that?

Selanio:
You know. The honeymoon suite.

Selan:
Heart-shaped beds?

Selanio:
It's more about what you do *on* the beds.

(Damon blushes. Selanio laughs.)

Selanio:
See, he knows what I'm talking about!

Xeno:
Don't be so crass.

Damon:
Well, I am anxious to leave, but more to get away from everyone here than… you know.

Clovis:
You don't have to lie to us, man. We don't judge what a guy does with his wife.

Damon (blushing more):
Um...

Selan:
Stop teasing him. =<

Selanio:
Heh. **(He notices a waiter walk by with a tray full of wine glasses.)** So *that's* where all the booze is coming from! HEY! Waiter! Gimme some wine!

(Xeno and Selan look at each other in horror, then both call to the waiter.)

Xeno and Selan (in unison):
No!

Selan:
No wine here, please!

Xeno:
Just ignore our friend here!

Selanio:
I hate you guys!

Clovis:
What, he an alcoholic or something?

Selan:
Not as such...

Xeno:
We just don't care to see him drunk.

Selan:
EVER. AGAIN. >_<

Damon:
Why? What happened last time?

Selanio:
Nothing bad!

Xeno:
He dropped his pants.

Selan:
	In public!

Xeno:
	It was so embarrassing.

Selan:
	It was scary ;o;

Selanio:
	You all are just intimidated by the glory of Selanio without his pants. u_u

Damon:
	O-okay…

Clovis:
	Get over yourself, man. -_-; No one wants to see a giant Russian man's bits.

Selanio:
	The ladies do.

Xeno:
	But WE don't.

Selan:
	And I don't either. =<

Damon:
	So, changing the subject…

Clovis:
	Yes, please. -_-;; So Damon. How's business?

Damon:
	-_-; Awful. My brother made a mess of everything and it's been difficult putting things back in order.

Selanio:
	Boring…

Xeno:
	You haven't had any trouble with the law, have you?

Damon:
	No, thankfully my new lawyer has been very good at pointing all the blame at Dalix. But…

Clovis:
But?

Damon:
He asks worrying questions.

Xeno:
About what?

(Dorcia has walked over by now, and she sits down next to Damon.)

Dorcia:
About the fact that people like myself and mister Fordon work for Damon.

Damon (talking in hushed tones):
Yes, that. Of course we keep everyone's powers under wraps, but he claims to have heard rumors. He won't leave the subject alone. I think he is worried about getting in trouble for working for us if we get caught, but…

Dorcia:
It is rather bothersome. -_-

Selanio (frowning):
Humor Selanio for a moment. What's this lawyer's name?

Damon:
Annick Zitomira. Why?

Selanio (pounding a fist on the table):
Son of a bitch! *You* hired him?!

Selan:
Selanio, lower your voice!

Selanio:
You're the reason Stesha's back! Gods*dammit!!*

Damon:
I'm confused.

Xeno:
Selanio here has a bit of a bad history with your lawyer's son. -_-;

Damon:
Oh. I apologize.

Xeno:
There's nothing to apologize for, really. Selanio's just a jackass.

Selanio:
Fuck you!

Selan (terrible with names):
Where has Selan heard the name Stesha before…?

Dorcia:
As riveting as this conversation is… Damon, they are expecting you to make a speech soon.

Damon (looking at his watch):
And then we leave, yes?

Dorcia:
Yes.

Damon:
Finally. **(He stands up.)** It has been nice seeing you all again. Thank you for coming.

Selan:
Selan would go anywhere for cake like this. =T

Selanio:
I hate you so much. >_<

Damon:
Ah… right. I'll just be going.

(Damon walks off to the front of the room to make his speech. Dorcia shoots glares at the inhabitants of the table—Selanio especially—and follows her husband. Selanio huffs, snatches a glass of wine off of a passing waiter's tray and chugs it down.)

Selanio:
Hah. u_u Take that, losers.

Xeno (sighing):
Whatever… **(He takes a glass of wine too.)**

Selan (not drinking age, not fond of wine):
Buu… =<

-End: Episode thirty-four.

035. Not this again...

(Tavvy, Marika and Audi are in the Professor's office on a Wednesday evening. Audi's reading some teenybopper magazine, the Professor is grading papers and Tavvy's looking annoyed.)

Marika:
Just answer the question.

Tavvy:
I don't see why I have to memorize that stuff. I mean, I have all these classes and tests to study for and you want me to learn the names of all these villains that aren't even around anymore.

Marika (writing something on a paper in red ink):
It's important to know your history, Tavarius. Everything I've taught you comes from my experience with these villains, and some of them, while inactive, are still at large. Who knows when they might return.

Tavvy:
If they return. And if they do I can ask you about it *then.* Can't I go home? I'm tired.

Marika:
Not unless you promise me you'll study.

Tavvy:
It isn't like there's a textbook or anything on this stuff!

Marika:
There are some useful Wikipedia articles.

Audi:
I edited them myself! **(She flips a page in her magazine.)**

Tavvy:
Hff…

Marika:
We'll try it this way. I'll try naming the villains and you tell me about them.

Tavvy:
Okay…

Marika:
Gamma and Beta.

Tavvy:
Uhn… they were a mad scientist pair. With lame names. Gamma was… the chick? Yeah. She was the chick, and Beta was the guy. You arrested them ages ago.

Audi (writing in pencil in her magazine):
But Gamma got away, so who knows if she'll ever come back.

Tavvy:
Yeah. That.

Marika:
And they're important to you, why…?

Tavvy:
Because… they're a lot like Quantum and Chandra?

Marika:
There you go. What about Reza?

Tavvy:
Oh, umm… he was… he was that nutjob, yeah?

Marika:
I wouldn't describe him that way.

Tavvy:
Oh. Well, he was that guy who bust a bunch of old villains out of jail. **(He pauses to think.)** He didn't just hang around here. He showed up in a lot of towns, pretty much anyplace that had a decent amount of superpowered people. He was trying to build an army, I think? But no one stuck around him for long. Umm… **(He tries to think of something else.)**

Marika (sighing):
Audi, help him out.

Audi:
His powers involved the ability to shoot spooky black energy bolts, which he could also arrange into shields, and limited flight. He was very powerful, daddy had a hard time taking him down. He was some sort of super-people's-rights activist, had a habit of preaching about how superpowered people were being oppressed and how they should rise up and yadda yadda yadda. Appeared all over the continental US and Canada, plus some sightings in England and various other places in Europe, reaching as far as Russia. **(She writes a little more in her magazine.)** Hey Tavvy, you wanna take a quiz about your relationship habits?

Tavvy:
Uh… no thanks.

Marika:
It's very sad how my fifteen-year-old daughter has this memorized and you, Tavarius, barely know it at all.

Tavvy:
But she's your *daughter!* Of course she knows all this, I'm sure you've been telling her these stories all her life!

Marika:
I rarely speak of my hero career with her.

Audi:
'strue.

Tavvy:

It's not like I watched the news as a kid, I didn't follow this stuff…

Audi:

You know what I think, daddy?

Marika:

Hm?

Audi:

I think this is just proof that I would make a great superhero.

Marika:

Not this again…

Audi:

Cuz, you know, I'm just as strong as Tavvy and I can take a punch too. I mean, I'm not super-fast and I don't have laser eye beams but I'd make a good sidekick, don't you think?

Marika:

How many times am I going to have to say this? No. **(He writes on another paper.)**

Audi:

Pleeaaase?

Marika:

No.

Tavvy:

You know, I really wouldn't mind the help. And if she's just a sidekick she doesn't have to worry about being there all the time, so if you have a curfew for her she could still—

Marika:

Absolutely *not.*

Audi:

Why not?

Marika:

It's no work for a girl your age.

Audi:

But Quantum looks my age and he's a villain, so why can't I be a hero?

Marika:

I'm sure his parents would disapprove if they knew, too.

Audi:

It's not fair…

Marika:

I don't care whether it's fair or not. This conversation is over.

Audi:

But—

Marika:

I said over. Tavarius, go home and study.

Tavvy:

-_-; Yes, sir…

(Tavvy gets up and starts walking toward the door, relieved to have finally been dismissed.)

Marika:

Oh, and…

Tavvy:

Yes…?

Marika:

Expect a very thorough test this weekend. You really seem to be slacking in both your studies and your training. I ought to do something about that.

Tavvy (groaning):

Aw, jeez, Professor…

Marika:

I'll hear no arguments. Now get going.

(Tavvy sighs and leaves.)

Audi:

Maybe if I was just a part-time sidekick… on the

weekends, maybe?

(The Professor shoots Audi a glare, and she sighs and returns to her magazine.)

Audi:
Never mind…

-End: Episode thirty-five.

036. You oddball...

(It's a school day, and Selan and Selanio are eating lunch outside on the green in front of one of the campus's larger dorms.)

Selan:
So, **(she eats a french fry)** how'd your test go?

Selanio:
Too easy. **(He takes a bite of a hamburger.)**

Selan:
What subject was it? One of your chem classes?

Selanio:
Yeah.

Selan:
Selan is jealous. Selan took chem in high school and it was so hard then. =< I don't know how you manage to do college-level stuff.

Selanio:
Selanio is a genius, you know that. u_u

Selan:
So it's almost time to apply for grad school.

Selanio:
Da.

Selan:
You gonna do it?

Selanio:
Nye znayu…

Selan:
You gotta decide soon, you don't wanna miss out.

Selanio:
I know, I know.

Selan:
Selan's so gonna go to grad school when the time comes. u_u You don't wanna get stuck with less of a degree than me, eh?

Selanio:
Hah, Selanio should go for his doctorate. Then I can be *Doctor* Roselani.

Selan:
Do it! Do it!

Selanio:
Selanio would have to dip into his stash though. My scholarships are running out.

Selan:
Your stash is huuuuuge. You've got like a bajillion diamonds lying around somewhere.

Selanio:
Selanio would hate to spend it on something boring like school…

Selan:
But you'll earn it all back being a big fancy doctorman.

Selanio:
Meh…

Selan:
Well, *I* think it'd be worth it.

Selanio:
I know you do.

(He takes another bite of his hamburger, but notices something and nearly chokes.)

Selan:
Eh? Selanio, remember to chew!

Selanio:
Ugh—shut up >_O Selanio knows to chew, it's just—

(Stesha walks up to the two of them.)

Selanio:
Just that. -_-;

Stesha:
Hey there. n_n

Selan:
Ah! I know I've seen you before. Where have I seen you before?

Stesha:
The burger place, remember? I didn't know you were friends with Selanio.

Selan:
You know him too?

Selanio:
Yes. -_O We know each other.

Selan (noticing the tone to Selanio's voice):
Er…

Stesha (sitting down with them):
What a delightful coincidence. n_n

Selanio:
… Selan, didn't you have a class to get to?

Selan:
Not for another… **(Selanio glares at Selan, and she**

pretends to look at a watch she doesn't have.) … oh, look at the time, you're right.

Selanio:
That's what I thought. u_u

Stesha:
Oh, well I guess it wouldn't be right to skip it…

Selan:
That's right! =D;;; See you guys later.

(She leaves.)

Stesha (watching her leave):
Hmm. So, I suppose that's your current girlfriend?

Selanio:
Of course not!

Stesha:
Oh? Well then. I suppose she really isn't your type anyway.

Selanio:
What's THAT supposed to mean? -_O

Stesha:
Nothing, never mind.

Selanio:
-_-; What the hell do you want, Zitomira?

Stesha:
What sort of question is that? We're old friends, I've just come back into town… I wanted to catch up is all.

Selanio:
Selanio believes that *completely*.

Stesha:
Is something the matter?

Selanio:
Look, I want you to stay away from Selan.

Stesha:
Hm? Why's that?

Selanio:

You *know* why! I know your history with women and I'll tell you now that you won't be able to add her to your list of conquests so I don't even want to see you try! Ti ponimayesh?

Stesha (shaking his head, still smiling):

Honestly, Selanio, sometimes I wonder if you're a bit too paranoid…

Selanio:

Selanio knows how this goes and won't watch it again! If I see you making any moves on her, I will personally beat you into a bloody pulp. This is a promise.

Stesha:

Okay, okay. n_n; Oh, Selanio, you oddball…

Selanio:

Hff. Anyway, Selanio is going to leave now.

Stesha:

Oh? Do you have a class now too?

Selanio:

It really isn't your business.

Stesha:

Oh, well…

Selanio:

Selanio assumes that you'll be just fine throwing out our trash, yes?

(He picks up his bag and puts it on over his shoulder.)

Stesha:

n_n;; Of course…

(Selanio walks off, leaving Stesha with all of his and Selan's lunch trash. Stesha groans, rolling his eyes, and starts to pick up their mess.)

-End: Episode thirty-six.

037. That hardly ever happens!

(It's the weekend! Selan and Selanio are at the mall. Selanio's sitting in one of the chairs in front of the fitting rooms in the women's section of a clothing store, looking bored out of his mind. Selan is in the fitting room, but presently she steps out and spins around.)

Selan:
How does Selan look?

Selanio:
Meh.

Selan:
Does my ass look okay?

Selanio:
It's hideous.

Selan:
You aren't even looking.

Selanio:
Just buy the pants, already.

Selan:
I need to know if they look good!

Selanio:
Look, they fit don't they? Just buy them.

Selan:
Not unless they look good! Selan hates pant shopping too, you know, this would be so much easier if you'd just tell me if my ass looks okay.

Selanio:
Well I'm not gonna. u_u;

Selan:
Whyyy?

Selanio:
Because your ass defies so many laws of Euclidean geometry that it would drive anyone who looks at it insane. It's like something out of Lovecraft.

Selan (looking back, trying to get a good look at her butt):
You're making it up.

Selanio:
It's true.

Selan:
How would you even know? You won't look.

Selanio:
See, this is a trap and Selanio isn't falling for it.

Selan:
Don't be stubborn.

Selanio:
Selanio values his sanity, thank you!

Selan:
Stop being such a jerk!

(Xeno walks over, carrying a bag of newly-bought clothes.)

Xeno:
What's Selanio doing now?

Selan:

He won't tell me if my butt looks okay!

Xeno:

Why would he do that?

Selan:

Cuz I *asked.*

Selanio:

It's a traaaaaap.

Xeno:

You know, Selan, it's kind of awkward for you to ask him to look at your butt.

Selan:

He looks at girls' butts all the time. He knows butts, he's a good guy to ask about this stuff!

Selanio:

I can't look at your butt, you're my friend.

Selan:

But I asked! You have permission!

Selanio:

You *asked* me about your boobs, too, and you—

Selan:

I asked about their size, I didn't say "Hey Selanio, grab my boobies!"

Selanio:

See, see? TRAP.

Xeno:

Look, Selan, if he doesn't want to look at your butt he doesn't have to. End of story.

Selan:

But… but… TToTT How will I tell if my butt looks okay?

Xeno:

It doesn't matter. -_-;

Selan:

Buuuut…

Xeno:

Just hurry up already, I wanna get some lunch.

Selan:

Buuuuut! TToTT

Selanio:

Stop going on about your butt, already! >_< I'll look, already, just shut up.

Selan:

Yaaaay, thanks! **(She turns around so Selanio can see her backside.)** Yeah? Yeah?

Selanio:

You look fat. u_u

Selan:

Whaaaaaat!

Xeno:

Goddammit, Selanio. >_<

Selan:

Stop lying! =O I'm ten pounds underweight and you know it! Now gimme an honest opinion!

Selanio:

You look fine. u_u Now can we go get food?

Selan:

I do?

Selanio:

Yes, yes.

Selan:

Pravda?

Selanio:

>_< Da! Pravda! Now let's go!

Selan:

Okay! =D

(She rushes into the fitting room to change back into the clothes she came in with.)

(Selanio and Xeno stand, waiting. A clock ticks. Xeno crosses his arms.)

Xeno:
So is there a reason why you're blushing?

Selanio:
Selanio is not blushing.

Xeno:
Your face is bright red, man.

Selanio:
You're full of *lies.*

Xeno:
Whatever…

(Selan comes out of the dressing room, carrying the pants she tried on.)

Selan:
Okay~~ Let's pay for these and get some delicious delicious mall-Chinese foods.

Selanio:
Finally.

(They go to the checkout and pay for the pants, and are soon sitting outside the mall eating food they got at the food court.)

Selanio:
So when's our next big heist, eh?

Selan (shrugging):
I dunno. Selan's been so busy with classes she hasn't had time to plan anything.

Xeno:
I could always check on when Quantum's doing stuff. That always seems to be a good time to do our thing.

Selanio:
But then I don't get to beat up Apogee.

Selan:
You mean, you don't get to have Apogee beat the

living tar out of you? That guy's been getting better at dispatching you, man.

Selanio:
Yeah, right.

Xeno:
Maybe you should spend some more time training? I'm sure that's what Apogee's been doing.

Selanio:
Groan… but to train Selanio has to go all the way to the abandoned trainyard and it's so far away. -_-;

Selan:
We could all come with you. =3 I'm sure Xeno wouldn't mind practicing too, plus I could cheer you on.

Selanio:
You could always do a little working out yourself.

Selan:
Whaaaat! I get enough physical activity in fights. I don't need any more.

Xeno:
You *are* pretty out of shape. Maybe if you ran laps you wouldn't get tired so easily…

Selan:
Exercise is for squares, man! =O

Selanio:
No, what's for squares is you not being able to use your barriers right because you're too easily exhausted.

Selan:
That hardly ever happens!

Selanio:
But it *does* happen.

Selan:
Hff…

Xeno:
So it's settled then. Let's do it tomorrow, since I'm working all next week and I'll be too tired for any working

out. -_-;

Selan:
But I don’t wanna. TToTT

Selanio (giving Selan a noogie):
Too bad, loser.

Selan:
I’m gonna destroooy youuu. =<

-End: Episode thirty-seven.

038. I think you broke him

(It's the next day! The three are out of town at the old abandoned trainyard. Selanio's been lifting trains all day, Xeno's been throwing trains at Selanio for him to catch, and Selan... well...)

Selanio:
Stop being so damn lazy.

Selan:
I'm noooot! −<

Selanio:
You're already wearing your workout clothes and everything, so just work out already.

Selan:
I don't wannaaaa!

Xeno:
Stop with the whiny voice. -_-;

Selanio:
Look, look, Selanio has a plan.

Selan:
Selan knows what it is!

Selanio:
What?

Selan:
You're gonna change your persona from Baron von Boom to SHIRTLESS MAN. It will be particularly useful against female and gay male superheroes.

Selanio:
… >_< What.

Selan:
I'm just sayin'. Put a damn shirt on.

Selanio:
Shush. Selanio's going to be brilliant.

Selan:
Is that possible?

Xeno:
Nope.

Selanio:
Shut up already. -_O Selan, you know how that one time, you made a barrier and pushed me with it?

Selan:
Yeah. Cuz you were gettin' squished by Clovis.

Selanio:
We need to have you practice doing that more. u_u

Selan:
But it's so hard to do =<

Selanio:
And this is why you're going to practice. u_u

Selan:
Fuu… okay, Selan will try it.

(Selan puts out her arms and makes a face like she's concentrating really hard. She makes a barrier. It sort of… sits there.)

Selanio:
It's not moving.

Selan:
Sure it is!

Xeno:
It really isn't.

Selanio:
Oh come on, you've done it once before, you should know how to do it!

Selan:
Selan was full of adrenaline at the time! I don't remember how I did it!

Selanio:
Sheesh. Okay, put the barrier down for a second.

(Selan complies. Selanio walks up and proceeds to lift Selan up off the ground)

Selan:
H-hey! Let go!

Selanio:
You're just gonna have to push me away with your barrier. u_u

Selan:
But I can't make them that close to me! Plus you're holding my arms down, jerk!

Selanio (shaking Selan around):
Less talk, more results~

Selan:
Meeeeeep! >_< Stop it, I'm getting dizzy!

Selanio:
I don't see any barriers~

Selan:
Eeeeeeeeeeep~!

Xeno:
Hey, put her down, she's starting to do that annoying

whining thing again.

(Xeno starts to walk over, but suddenly Selan manages to make a barrier which appears, shoots forward, smacks Xeno in the face, and breaks. Xeno rubs his forehead.)

Xeno:

… ow.

Selanio:

Hah! I'm a GENIUS.

Selan:

Put me down now, yes yes? ;o;

Selanio:

Sure. **(He sets Selan back down on the ground and walks over to Xeno.)** Hey, did she break anything?

Xeno:

No, I'm okay.

Selanio:

Too bad.

Xeno:

Ass.

Selanio (turning to face Selan again):

Okay, now if we can just—

(Selan tries mimicking what she just accidentally did. Another barrier appears, expands, and hits Selanio square in the nose. He falls over. Selan gasps.)

Selan:

Sorry! I didn't mean to make it go out that far! =<

Xeno:

Serves you right.

(Selanio sits up, groaning. He puts a hand to his nose, and finds it's bleeding.)

Selan (hoping she hasn't invoked Selanio's wrath):

You okay?

(Selanio pops his broken nose back into place, and proceeds

to start laughing.)

Xeno:
I think you broke him, Selan. He's crazier than normal now.

Selan:
Oh noes, and here I don't have the squirrel with me.

Selanio:
Shut up, you two, and pay attention to the implications here!

Xeno:
What implications?

Selanio:
With this, Selan might actually not be so damn useless!

Selan:
Hey, I'm useful!

Xeno:
She isn't useless, Selanio, she's saved your life more times than I can count.

Selanio:
But she can't do a bit of damage to anyone so she's useless in a fight. u_u We know this! But once she gets the hang of this thing, she might actually be able to hurt something.

Selan:
I can damage people, I've got kunai, and…

Selanio:
How often do you actually hit anything with those, really? -_O

Selan:
Well, er…

Selanio:
See! But now you can, like… jeez, you could probably crush people against walls and stuff! How badass is that?

Selan:
I was badass before though.

Selanio:
Heh.

Selan:
That wasn't a joke!

Xeno:
Is your nose gonna be okay?

Selanio (wiping some blood off his face):
Yeah, Selanio breaks his nose all the time. I'll just take a nap while you're driving us home, it'll be better in no time.

Selan:
Does Selanio need some ibuprofen?

Selanio:
No. Now keep practicing! I want you to be able to do that in your sleep by the time we're done here!

Selan:
=< What's all this, you're talking like you're the boss.

Selanio:
I'm the boss of working out. u_u I declare it.

Xeno:
Isn't that the sort of thing we should vote on?

Selanio (standing up):
There is no voting in exercise! Now Xeno—come throw some more trains at me! Selan—keep doing that thing!

Selan:
Meeeh…

Xeno:
Fine, fine… -_-;;

-End: Episode thirty-eight.

039. Nice shot.

(The scene is our villains' house. The three are just coming in from their latest battle against the forces of good and while they all look rather worse for wear, they seem pleased.)

Baron von Boom:
See! I told you! Selan is one hundred percent less useless!

Lady Ira:
Shut up, I'm just as useful as always.

Omen (taking off his scarf):
Actually, Selanio, we probably did better because you worked out… not that Selan's new trick didn't help.

Baron von Boom:
While Selanio is eager to point out that yes, I did do most of the work, I must say that it's amazing actually having Selan not standing in the back doing nothing all the time.

Lady Ira:
Selan is tiring of all the backhanded compliments. -.-;

Omen:
It was pretty cool when she knocked Apogee at you.

Baron von Boom:
That was freaking amazing! Hah! How much money did we manage to make off with, anyway?

Lady Ira (emptying her pockets):
I've got, umm… about two thousand, maybe?

Omen (also emptying his pockets):
Thirty two hundred. Selanio?

Baron von Boom (counting out his loot):
Odinnatset, dvyenatset… uhn. Thirteen hundred. Too bad Apogee wrestled the moneybag off me.

Lady Ira:
Good thing he didn't notice we'd stuffed our pockets.

Omen:
Seriously. But I guess I'd call that a successful heist. We made off with some decent loot, managed to rough Apogee up a bit, and… er… **(He catches sight of the clock.)** Shit, it's that late already?

(He runs to his room to get changed.)

Lady Ira:
Oh noes, is it time for work?

Baron von Boom:
Just call in sick, man! We've gotta celebrate! This is the best we've done in months!

Xeno (rushing out, pulling on his jacket):
We pull off a heist and then I don't come to work? Yeah, that doesn't look suspicious at all! Sorry guys, I value my secret identity!

Lady Ira:
Should we wait for you to come back before we celebrate?

Xeno:

Whatever! Don't care! Bye! **(He runs out the door.)**

Baron von Boom:

Pfft. Loser. Why's he even have that job anyway? We've got enough ill-gotten gains to pay the bills.

Lady Ira:

Cuz it looks suspicious if none of us have jobs but still manage to pay for the house and all.

Baron von Boom:

Whatever. Let's go have fun without him.

Lady Ira:

Aww, but that's not nice.

Baron von Boom:

We're villains. u_u We aren't nice. Let's go spend some money at least.

Lady Ira:

Can we go to the mall? =D

Baron von Boom:

Ugh...

Lady Ira:

No clothes stores this time, I promise! Video games and useless stuff, all the way!

Baron von Boom:

Sure, fine.

Lady Ira:

Yay!

(The two go to their rooms to change back into their civilian clothes. They get into Selanio's car and drive down to the mall. Pretty soon they're in the game store, looking at the latest releases.)

Selan:

Selan wonders if this one is good.

Selanio:

So buy it and find out.

Selan:

But Selan doesn't want to waste money if it sucks. =<

Selanio:

-_- What's it matter? You've got plenty.

Selan:

I guess… are you getting anything?

Selanio (shrugging):

Maybe.

Selan:

What is it? **(She looks over to see what Selanio's holding)** Is that a Kirby game?

Selanio:

Nyet… >_>

Selan:

I already have that one, man! You could just borrow it.

Selanio:

Selanio doesn't want to borrow it!

Selan:

I didn't even realize you play Kirby games. I mean, Kirby's such a cute little thing and you're… *you.*

Selanio:

Selanio doesn't!

Selan:

You don't have to be embarrassed.

Selanio:

I'm not. u_u I just don't want to play such a lame game!

Selan:

Then why're you holding the box?

Selanio:

>_>…

Selan (giggling):

You know what? Selan will just go outside and sit on

that bench there and I won't pay aaaany attention to what game you buy.

Selanio:
Shut up! =O

Selan:
Here I go~

(Selan wanders off. A few minutes later, Selanio comes out carrying a bag and looking annoyed.)

Selan (Kirby voice):
Hiiii~

Selanio:
Shut up. >_<

Selan:
Aww, it's okay Selanio, lots of macho guys like Kirby games.

Selanio:
Hey, here's an idea, let's stop talking about that game I didn't buy.

Selan:
Sure you did, the bag's right there!

Selanio (pulling a violent-looking game out of the bag):
Did not. u_u

Selan:
Looks like something else is in there…

Selanio (putting the game back):
There is not. u_u

Selan:
Okay, okay. Hey, what's over there?

(She wanders off again.)

Selanio (following her):
You have a short attention span, you know that?

Selan:
They didn't have this before. It's one of those photo

booth things.

Selanio:
So?

Selan:
I've never done one of these things. You wanna try it?

Selanio:
Why do I have to be involved?

Selan:
Stuff like this is boring alone. C'mooon, I'll pay for it!

Selanio:
Fine, whatever…

(The two get in the photo booth. After putting money in and fiddling with the settings, they get their pictures taken and get out. They wait at the side of the machine for it to give them their photos.)

Selanio:
What is it with girls and photo booths?

Selan:
Hm?

Selanio:
Every time Selanio is on a date with a girl and she sees a photo booth, she goes "Ooh, I've never done one of these before, let's get our picture taken!"

Selan:
One of them has gotta be lying.

Selanio:
Either that or they're just so eager to get pictures of my gorgeous self that they would bother with these pointless things. u_u

Selan:
Oh, of course. **(Nod, nod.)**

(The machine spits out their photos. Selan takes them and the two of them take a look.)

Selan:
We look silly.

Selanio:
Your face looks silly.

Selan:
Your *mom* looks silly.

Selanio:
You can keep the pictures. Selanio needs no photos of someone whose face he keeps seeing all the time.

Selan:
Selan can use Photoshop to put your face on stuff! =3

Selanio:
-_O...

Selan:
I kid, I kid.

(Later, they're passing by the food court. They notice that one of the mall workers is emptying the pennies out of the fountain. Selanio's face lights up and he nudges Selan.)

Selanio:
Hey, follow me!

Selan:
What about food?

Selanio:
Later!

(The two of them run up the escalator to the second floor. Selanio leans over the railing, pulls a penny out of his pocket, and throws it at the worker in the fountain. It hits the guy square on the head.)

Selan:
Nice shot.

Selanio:
Look away.

(The guy looks up to see who threw the penny, and Selan and Selanio both look away, pretending not to have noticed.

Eventually he returns to his work, and Selanio fishes another penny out of his pocket. He continues throwing small change at the worker until a security guard notices them and calls out. Selanio looks up at the guard making his way toward them, laughs, grabs Selan by the hand and runs off, dragging Selan along. Eventually they find themselves in a hallway a ways away, standing against a wall between the pay phones and the bathrooms, both of them laughing.)

Selan:

You know, he probably wasn't going to do anything. He probably would've just told you to cut it out.

Selanio:

No, no, you're wrong. He knew who we were, see! And he realized that if he caught us he'd finally be promoted to something other than lowly mall cop and thought that he stood a chance against our might!

Selan (laughing more):

Oh, the hubris!

Selanio (also laughing):

The folly of the mall cop.

Selan:

Now can we get something to eat?

Selanio:

Sure. But let's leave and go to a real restaurant for once.

Selan:

Okay =T

-End: Episode thirty-nine.

040. Yawn.

(It's morning, and Apogee's flying high through the sky—not over the city, though, but rather he's traveling somewhere. He's been flying for a while, as his weary expression would indicate. But where is he going? Hmmm…)

(Wavy flashback! It's about an hour ago, and Tavvy's just been called to Professor Marika's office.)

Tavvy:
What's going on, Professor?

Marika:
I just got a message for you. Here.

(He hands Tavvy a fax printout.)

Tavvy (reading it):
The… the president's been kidnapped?

Marika:
That in itself is nothing special. It happens. Look at which villain's doing it.

Tavvy:

… *Reza?* This guy's been retired for years!

Marika:

Not retired, *inactive*. There's a crucial difference. In any case, they want you to go to DC and help rescue him.

Tavvy:

Isn't there already a hero working that area?

Marika:

Yes, but since this is a delicate situation they are calling for backup. You should feel honored, Tavarius. The powers that be are beginning to take you seriously.

Tavvy:

Hnn…

Marika:

That paper has the location you are to meet with the other heroes at. Leave immediately.

Tavvy:

… but you aren't coming?

Marika:

I remind you that I'm retired. Now go on.

(Back in the present, Tavvy's landing at a secluded warehouse just outside the city. He enters and looks around, not seeing anyone. He walks farther in.)

Apogee:

Hellooo?

(Someone covers Apogee's eyes.)

???:

Guess who.

Apogee:

Uh… another hero, I hope?

???:

Nah, man, obviously I'm some sort of horrible villain out to kill you. But, you know, I'm not gonna be smart and stab you in the back or anything, no.

(The person lets go of Apogee. Apogee turns around, scratching his head awkwardly.)

Apogee:
But they never do anything logical like stabbing me in the back. Not even when they have the chance.

Other hero:
Point taken. Okay, I'm Ohm. Good to see you again, Tavvy.

Apogee (confused):
Have we met?

Ohm:
What, don't tell me you don't remember! I met you last year when I was visiting my cousin Cathal.

Apogee (staring incredulously):
… *Tynan?!*

Ohm:
There you go.

Apogee:
I didn't realize you were a superhero!

Ohm:
I didn't know you were either. Funny how these things work out.

Apogee:
This is so weird! Does—does Cath realize you're…?

Ohm:
Of course. What, does he know about you?

Apogee:
No.

Ohm:
You sure about that?

Apogee:
I'm pretty sure… why?

Ohm:
Cath's a sneaky bastard. He tends to find out about

things and then pretend like he doesn't know. Like this one time when I was 15, I was going out with this girl and my parents didn't like her so I didn't want anyone to know I was with her, right? So like a year after I dumped her, I find out Cath had known the whole time and he'd acted like he didn't.

Apogee:
I've been really careful about my secret identity… I'm *pretty* sure Cath doesn't know anything.

Ohm:
All right, if you say so…

Apogee:
Anyway, isn't there supposed to be anyone else here?

Ohm:
Well, I think Quentin's supposed to show up, but he's coming from farther away, so he isn't here yet…

Apogee:
Who?

Ohm:
Quentin Dace. Shockwave. Comes from up north.

Apogee:
Sounds familiar… I think he might be a friend of the Professor's?

Ohm:
Yeah, apparently the two worked together on a few missions. I don't like the guy, personally. He's got a stick up his ass or something.

Apogee:
I wonder why so many heroes that're that old are so uptight.

Ohm:
Probably something wrong with their generation in general.

Apogee:
Or maybe it's something to do with being a hero for so long.

Ohm:

God, I hope not. Could you please kill me if I start acting like that?

Apogee:

Ah… sure? ^^;

(The door opens and another hero—Shockwave, presumably—walks in. He looks over the other two.)

Shockwave:

Is this all? Just you two?

Ohm:

Oh I know, you're just *so* excited to work with us! Let's get going.

Shockwave:

Fine…

(They walk outside. Apogee approaches Shockwave.)

Apogee:

Ah… I'm Apogee.

Shockwave:

Pavel's apprentice. I know.

Apogee:

I-it's nice meeting you.

Shockwave:

Is it? I'll reserve judgment until I've seen you in action.

Apogee:

Hum…

(The three start flying—Apogee and Shockwave with their jetpacks, and Ohm with the aid of an oblong metal disc he stands on and manipulates with his electromagnetic powers.)

Shockwave:

So what is the plan?

Ohm:

Reza's already revealed his position and invited us over. What's gonna happen is you're gonna sneak in the back and secure the president while Apogee and I keep the psycho busy.

Shockwave:
Can I actually trust you children with holding off one of the country's most dangerous villains?

Apogee:
Don't worry, Mister Shockwave. Ohm and I can do it.

Ohm:
It's no sweat. We've got him outnumbered.

Shockwave:
Don't get overconfident.

Ohm:
Pfft. 9_9 Don't you go getting too optimistic.

(They arrive at where the President is being held, a small abandoned house a few miles away from the warehouse. There's no huge crowd of police around the place like Apogee would have expected, but Ohm quietly informs the others that the area is full of secret service agents, hiding in various places nearby.)

Apogee:
That's comforting.

Ohm:
Not really. Those guys may be great against your usual criminals and terrorists, but they're not much more than collateral damage against a guy like this.

Shockwave:
I don't suppose they would leave if we asked.

Ohm:
You know they won't.

Shockwave:
Let's get this over with…

(Shockwave walks off, heading to the other side of the building. Ohm looks at Apogee.)

Ohm:
You ready?

(Apogee nods, and Ohm kicks down the door. The two rush in.)

Ohm:
Surrender, Reza!

Apogee:
We have you surrounded!

(Instantly there's a flurry of movement—a wave of black energy shoots out at the two heroes, who both brace themselves. Apogee crouches down, relying on his invulnerability to protect him, and Ohm hides behind his flying disc, using it as a shield. Once the attack is over, the two look up to see Reza looming over them.)

Reza:
Hm. Not bad.

Apogee:
We're here to save the President.

Reza:
Obviously.

Ohm:
I'd recommend you just give up, man. It'll save you an ass-kicking.

Reza:
Is that so.

Apogee:
Yeah. And the courts might go easy on you if you don't fight us.

Reza:
Hm. **(He yawns.)** Forgive me for not caring, but you must understand that I've heard all of this before from heroes much greater than you.

(Reza leaps forward, sending a wave of darkness at Ohm. Ohm dodges, but gets hit by a second barrage which sends him flying into a nearby pile of debris. Reza turns his sights on Apogee.)

Reza:
Tell me, what is your name?

Apogee (clenching his fists):
I'm Apogee.

Reza:
Ah, yes, I thought you looked familiar. You're the good Professor's little protégé, aren't you? **(Black energy envelops his arm and he punches at Apogee, who blocks the blow.)** Yes, I thought as much. You know, it was the Professor who was the one to put me in jail. Luckily I escaped, but I'd always planned on taking revenge. But it's funny how life can get in the way sometimes.

(Reza charges another super-punch, but Ohm shoots a lightning bolt at Reza, who uses the energy on his arm to deflect the bolt instead. Reza swipes his hand out and a bolt of energy shoots out, then follows the motion of his hand to lash out at Apogee and then Ohm. Ohm blocks the attack with his shield, and Apogee jumps out of the way, sending himself on a jetpack-powered lunge at Reza. Reza catches Apogee's punch with one energized hand and blasts Apogee in the face with the other. Apogee flies across the room, hitting the wall, his face smoking and his goggles cracked.)

Apogee:
Th-these goggles are bullet-proof…

(Just then, Shockwave walks in from the other side of the room, cracking his knuckles.)

Shockwave:
It is over, Reza! The president has been freed, your plan is at its end.

Reza:
Hm. Tell me, you didn't actually think that I would leave the president unsupervised if I didn't expect you to free him, did you?

Ohm:
… *shit.*

(Suddenly a gunshot rings out, echoing loudly outside.)

Reza:
He was not worthy to rule this country. He was one of *them*, my fellows. Those weak ones should not be allowed to rule over beings as powerful as we.

(Ohm dashes for the door and throws it open, looking out to see what's happened. Meanwhile Reza grabs the dazed Apogee and throws him at Shockwave, who just barely manages to catch him.)

Ohm:
He—he's okay! One of the suits got him out of the way in time!

(Reza, by now, has turned his sights on Ohm, and has charged energy into his arms.)

Ohm:
Your plan's failed, Reza, you-

(Ohm turns to face the fray, only to find Reza right up in his face.)

Reza: You will regret having impeded me, all of you.

(Ohm gets a fistful of dark energy right in the chest—the energy releases upon impact, exploding outward and sending Ohm flying.)

Apogee (snapping out of his dazed state):
O-Ohm! **(He rushes at Reza and starts attacking, trying to keep the villain occupied.)** Shockwave! Go—

Shockwave:
Yes, I know. **(He runs to Ohm, looking over his injuries, then looks back at Apogee.)** We have to get him to a doctor.

Apogee:
Then go! Get him out of here! **(He just barely dodges a punch.)**

Shockwave:
You'll end up killed if I leave you alone, you fool.

Apogee:
I'll be fine!

(Shockwave sighs, rolls his eyes, and stands up. He walks over to the fight, pushes Apogee aside, and hits his fists together—this causes a massive shockwave that knocks Reza into a wall. Shockwave then continues making these shocks, now focusing them at the ground until the earth shakes and

the floor opens, causing Reza to fall into a newly-formed fissure. Shockwave makes one last shock, this one focused at the roof, causing a portion of it to collapse over the fissure and block it.)

Apogee:
… Wow.

Shockwave:
That will not hold him long. We must flee.

Apogee:
Couldn't you just—

Shockwave:
I had him by surprise—I know I cannot beat him alone in a fair fight. I have tried before and failed. If he causes any more trouble, then we can return and take care of him once Ohm is in the hands of a doctor. **(He picks Ohm up.)** Now run.

(The heroes run out from the ruined house, yelling at the remaining secret service agents to get out immediately before Reza could break free. Soon the three are flying away, with Shockwave still carrying Ohm. It isn't long before the fallen superhero comes to.)

Ohm (groaning):
Ffffuck… we won, right?

Shockwave:
In a manner of speaking.

Apogee:
We had to run away. But the President got away fine, so I guess it's mission success.

Ohm:
Yeah, except we'll have to deal with him again later… goddammit, this hurts… >_<

Shockwave:
Do not try to move. I'm not certain how bad your injuries are.

Ohm:
Ugh… this fucking sucks…

Apogee:
Yeah… I'm sorry, Mister Shockwave. I'm sure you're disappointed in us.

Shockwave:
We did the best that we were able. Conditions were not in our favor.

Apogee (having expected a Marika-style "YOU SUCK"):
R-really?

Shockwave:
But next time, please do not fail so miserably.

(Apogee and Ohm sigh. The three continue to fly away, leaving behind a villain that they know they must one day face again…)

-End: Episode forty.

041. That isn't swimming.

(It's the weekend, and our villains are at the beach! Yaaaay. Selan, Selanio and Xeno are all there, with Brian and Ann tagging along. They've just arrived there, and the boys are waiting as the girls are in the changing room putting on their bathing suits.)

Selanio:
Maaaan, what's taking them so long?

Xeno:
It looked like there was a line in there, when the door opened.

Brian:
What, were you peeking?

Xeno:
No.

Selanio:
Hah, Xeno's a pervert.

Xeno:
I am not! Besides, the girls change behind curtains,

so I wouldn't be able to see anything even if I DID look…

Selanio:
You know an awful lot about girls' changing rooms.

Xeno:
Shut up, Selanio!

Brian:
Yeah. There were curtains in the mens' room too, moron, the places are probably set up the same.

Selanio:
Well, Xeno was still peeking. u_u

Brian:
Yep.

Xeno:
You all suck. >_<

(Finally, the door opens and Selan and Ann walk out in their bathing suits. Selan's wearing a brown-and-blue two-piece 'tankini' with shorts as a bottom, and Ann's wearing a purple one-piece.)

Selanio:
Sheeesh. You two are like turtles.

Selan:
It's not our fault! All the other chicks were taking so freaking long.

Ann:
Yeah.

Brian (blushing):
Y-you look good in that swimsuit, Ann.

Ann:
You think so? n_n

Brian:
Y-yeah.

Selanio (snickering):
Watch out, kid, that means he's thinking IMPURE THOUGHTS about that bathing suit.

Brian:
Sh-shut up!

Selanio:
You see? You can tell it's true from how he denies it!

Brian:
I'm denying it because it *isn't* true, you jackass!

Xeno:
We've all been through puberty before, Brian, we know how it goes.

Brian:
Shut *up,* dammit!

Ann (sighing):
Boys…

Selan (rolling her eyes):
Seriously. **(Loudly and deliberately, so as to let the boys hear over their arguing)** Come on, Ann, let's go rub sunscreen on each other!

Ann (giggling):
Alright.

(The two girls walk down toward the beach, carrying their towels and sunscreen. The boys all look at each other. Xeno rolls his eyes.)

Xeno:
Does she think we'd really be bothered by that?

Brian (shrugging):
Whatever. Let's go.

Selanio:
Seriously. Selan is completely ridiculous. Come on.

(The three start following the girls)

Xeno:
You two are awfully eager. -_O

Selanio:
We have to make sure they don't get their skinny asses eaten by sharks.

Brian:
There aren't any sharks.

Selanio:
It's the ocean. Of *course* there are sharks.

(They get to the beach, and much merriment is had—mostly involving everyone splashing everyone else, kicking down sandcastles and overall having a lot of fun. The sun is low in the sky, however, when Xeno notices something…)

Xeno:
What the… **(He runs down to another part of the beach and finds Indrid sitting in very shallow water, looking straight forward toward the ocean with a lobster sitting on his face.)** Indrid?!

Indrid:
Greetings.

Xeno:
What are *you* doing here?

Indrid:
Swimming.

Xeno:
It doesn't *look* like you're swimming.

Indrid:
Oh, yes? What does it look like, then?

(Indrid glances over at Xeno—Xeno gets the distinct feeling that he should change the subject.)

Xeno:
… you do realize that there's a—

Indrid:
A lobster on my head. Yes. I know.

Xeno:
Is there any reason why there's a lobster on your head?

Indrid:
I suppose it decided that it would be comfortable there.

Xeno:
Okay…

(A blue-haired girl walks over from out in the water. She looks down at Indrid.)

Girl:
There you are. Why aren't you swimming?

Indrid:
I am swimming. Observe.

(He splashes the water around him a bit.)

Girl:
That isn't swimming.

Xeno:
Uh… Indrid? Who's this?

Indrid:
This is Zahra. She helps me with some of the work that I do. Zahra, this is Xenophon.

Zahra:
Pleased to meet you.

Xeno:
What, so is she an alien, too?

Indrid:
No.

Xeno:
So she's human?

Indrid:
No.

Xeno:
Okay…

Zahra:
Indrid, why is there a lobster on your head?

Indrid:
Perhaps that is a question you should ask the lobster.

Zahra (carefully picking up the lobster and putting it in the water):
I think it likes you.

Indrid:
Perhaps.

Xeno:
So you're not here for any particular reason?

Indrid:
I assume that by now, you see me as some sort of harbinger of misfortune?

Xeno:
Pretty much.

Indrid:
I assure you that I do other things with my time than just warn you of things.

Xeno:
But still, it's weird seeing you hanging out at the beach.

Zahra:
It was my idea, actually. I'm trying to teach him to swim.

Xeno:
… **(he tries not to laugh)** Y-you can't swim?

Indrid:
I can swim very well. Just not in this body.

Zahra:
He isn't very willing to learn though. -_-;

Indrid:
I have no need to swim here.

Xeno:
Somehow I feel better about myself.

(Indrid glances at Xeno again. Xeno laughs.)

Xeno:
I just can't get scared by that!

(Zahra ruffles Indrid's hair.)

Zahra:

Come on, Indrid, you'll get it eventually.

Xeno:

It's not like it's all that hard. It doesn't really take all that effort to float.

Indrid:

I have a higher molecular density than you do.

Zahra:

You're just making excuses, you're still buoyant enough. **(She tugs on his arm.)** Now come on!

(Indrid reluctantly gets up and allows Zahra to lead him by the arm into deeper waters. Xeno watches them go, blinks, and walks back to his friends.)

Selan:

Xeno looks like his brain just broke.

Xeno:

I think it just did. o_O

Selanio:

Good, maybe you won't be so boring now.

Xeno:

Dude, Indrid is over there, right?

Selanio:

He is? *Shit.*

Selan:

What's he doing here?

Xeno:

Swimming. But that's beside the point. The point is, *I think he has a girlfriend.*

Selan:

Whaaaaaat! What makes you think that? Did he say so?

Xeno:

No, but… I mean, he's with this girl, and something about the way she's acting around him makes it seriously look like something's going on.

Selan:
Aww, that's cute.

Selanio:
Hah! The creepy-ass alien weirdo is getting more than Xeno is!

Xeno:
I know! What the hell?!

Ann (walking over):
What's going on?

Selan:
Indrid has a girlfriend!

Ann:
Who's that?

Selanio:
Terrifying alien guy.

Selan:
He isn't *that* scary.

Ann:
Well anyway. Brian's building a bonfire so we can toast some marshmallows and stuff.

Selan:
Dude. We have marshmallows?

Ann:
Yeah. n_n Brian and I brought them.

Selanio:
You two made yourselves useful for once, nice.

Selan:
Don't be a jerk. … Oh! Hey, Xeno, go invite Indrid and his girlfriend to have marshmallows with us!

Xeno:
What?!

Selanio:
Yeah, are you nuts?!

Selan:
Selan wants to meet this girlfriend of his. Also it's good to be friendly with people who possess the wisdom of the cosmos.

Selanio:
The only wisdom he has is the wisdom of creeping me out!

Xeno:
Groan… alright, I'll go invite them.

Selanio (as Xeno walks off):
No! Don't do it! *You'll doom us all!*

Ann:
Is this guy really that scary?

Selan:
A little… But he's Xeno's sensei and he lives on the moon so he's cool.

Selanio:
Selanio is pretty sure Xeno has been anally probed by him.

Xeno (returning):
I have not, shut up.

Selan:
I'm sure not all aliens anally probe things, Selanio.

Xeno:
That's right.

Selan:
I mean, there are plenty of other places Xeno could've been probed.

Xeno:
That's—hey!

Selanio:
Selanio dares not imagine.

Selan:
So is he coming?

Xeno:
Yeah, as soon as they pull this squid off his leg. Apparently sea creatures *really* like him.

Selanio:
Can't imagine why.

(A little later, the sun is little more than a light spot on a dark horizon as our villains, plus Indrid and Zahra, sit around a bonfire. They're all eating marshmallows and sandwiches—except for Indrid, who just continues to hold his marshmallow over the fire as it burns to a charred, gooey mess. He seems to have no interest in actually eating it.)

Brian:
So Xeno actually *did* get his powers from aliens.

Xeno:
I told you.

Brian:
But how do I know you guys aren't just making it up? I mean, this guy looks weird but he could still be a normal human.

Selan:
We've been on his moon base! He's totally an alien.

Brian:
You could be lying too.

Xeno:
Look, Indrid doesn't lie.

Zahra:
That's right.

Brian:
Liars can claim not to lie.

Indrid:
Except that I am not claiming anything.

Xeno:
He's got a point.

Brian:
Whatever. So what'd they do to you, anyway, Xeno? Did they open up your skull and implant something, or use some sort of brainwashing, or…

Xeno:
It's not like I remember any of it.

Brian:
Did the aliens look like him?

Xeno:
I don't know, okay?

Selan:
Just make something up. Be all like, 'yeah Brian, these green tentacle monsters put a radioactive hamster in my head, my powers are powered by it running in a wheel.'

Brian:
Oh, ha ha.

Selanio:
Sounds about as plausible as anything else involving these weirdos. u_u … but I still maintain that his powers come from a probe in his butt.

Xeno:
I hate you so much, Selanio.

Selan:
So, hey! Zahra lady!

Zahra:
Hm? Yes?

Selan:
Are you and Indrid like boyfriend and girlfriend, lovey lovey kissy kissy?

Xeno:
>_< What are you, ten?

Zahra (blushing):
W-well, I—we—er…

Indrid:
Yes.

(Zahra blushes more)

Xeno:
What, seriously? You admit it just like that?

Indrid:
Why would I deny it?

Xeno:
Well firstoff, because of the inane way Selan phrased it—

Selan:
Heeeey.

Xeno:
And besides, haven't you got a reputation to keep?

Indrid:
No.

Zahra:
What would Indrid need with a reputation?

Xeno:
I don't know, I just thought… >_>;;… nevermind.

Selanio:
How can you stand to date this guy?

Zahra:
What?

Selanio:
Look at him! He's terrifying.

Zahra:
What are you talking about? Indrid's incredibly sweet.

(She leans on Indrid, hugging his arm)

Xeno (remembering how Indrid trained him…):
Sweet. Right.

Zahra:
He is! Really.

Xeno:

I believe you completely… 9_9

(And so the night continues on, the group sitting around the campfire talking and stuff, until it's late and our villains leave. Indrid and Zahra remain, sitting at the campfire alone, as the beach empties of all human life and the night draws to a close…)

-End: Episode forty-one.

042. My machine!

(Our villains are hanging out at Brian's secret lab, of all places. Ann invited them, of course. But while they're there, Brian's brought out his latest invention to show off…)

Selan (looking at it):
It's… a shiny thing!

Selanio:
It's probably something stupid. _ ;

Brian:
Shut up, all of you, and let me tell you what it does.

Ann:
It's really neat. n_n

Brian:
I'm sure none of you know anything about this sort of thing, but since Quantum mechanics is so weird, most things that people think are physically impossible are actually possible, just so improbable that they probably won't ever happen. Things like teleportation, or walking through walls… so I've made this machine. It can make improbable things

like that happen.

Selan:
So- wait, wait, wait.

Brian:
What? -_-;

Selan:
It's an infinite improbability drive?

Brian:
A what?

Selan:
You know, like in Hitchhiker's Guide.

Selanio:
Oh, lord… -_-

Ann:
Actually, it's more like a finite improbability generator.

Xeno:
So can it do that thing, making a person's underpants jump a foot to the left?

Ann:
It can!

Brian:
What are you all going on about? -_O

Selanio:
Hah, do it!

Ann:
Who to?

Selanio:
Do it to Xeno.

Selan:
No, do it to Selanio!

Selanio:
See, this won't work, as Selanio is not wearing

underpants. u_u

Xeno:

Ugh, too much information, man…

Selan:

Ew.

Brian:

Will you all shut the fuck up and tell me what you're all talking about?

Selan:

It's like Hitchhiker's Guide, man!

Brian:

And what's that supposed to be?

Selan:

GASP. You built a finite improbability generator and you haven't even read Hitchhiker's Guide?

Ann:

Well, I've read it at least.

Selan:

That's because you're cool. Brian, obviously, is some kind of loser.

Selanio:

Selanio hasn't read it either.

Selan:

Okay, Brian AND Selanio are some kind of losers.

Selanio:

Hey!

Brian:

Do you really have to put me on the same level as this moron? -_-;

Ann:

Here, Brian, just show them what it can do.

Selan:

Make us turn into little plush us-es!

Brian:

… considering that would probably kill you, I have no objections.

Ann:

Shush. Try entering in this probability factor.

(She hands him a slip of paper.)

Brian:

What's this?

Ann:

Just try it. n_n;

(Brian types in a long number and hits the green button. There's a flash of light, and all of a sudden the trashcan has become… a bowl of petunias?)

Brian:

… what was the point of that?

Ann:

I thought it would amuse Selan.

Selan:

But is it thinking, 'Oh no, not again'?

Ann:

And besides, it saves me the trouble of taking out the trash.

Brian:

Point taken.

Selanio:

Laaaaame.

Xeno:

Oh, I know!

(He goes over to Brian and whispers something to him. Brian laughs.)

Brian:

I can totally do that! One moment…

(He turns to his computer and starts typing, working out the

probability factors for whatever it was Xeno suggested)

Selan:
What'd you say?

Xeno:
You'll see. >)

Selanio:
It better be more interesting than stupid *flowers.* 9_9

Xeno:
Oh yes, much more interesting.

Brian:
Got it. Heheh…

(He types the number into the improbability generator and mashes 'go'. There's a flash of light, and…)

Selan:
… Where'd Selanio go?

Xeno (laughing):
Right there, look!

Selan:
Wh- **(She starts laughing too.)** Selanio is a squirrel!

(Indeed, our giant Russian friend has become… a small, black squirrel. Everyone in the room laughs. Squirrel-Selanio, though, seems less than amused—he immediately jumps on Xeno, scratches the hell out of his face, then jumps onto Brian's face and proceeds to do the same.)

Brian:
Ow! Ow! Fuck! OKAY, I'll change you back, ow!

(Squirrel-Selanio jumps back onto the ground and looks up at Brian with an impatient expression. Brian types something into the improbability generator, hits the green button and, with a flash, Selanio is returned to normal. He rushes forward and grabs both Brian and Xeno by the collars of their shirts.)

Selanio:
You sons of bitches! Don't you ever even fucking *dream* of doing something like that again, do you hear me?!

Selan:
Selanio, calm down!

Ann:
It was just a joke, there's no need to get so upset…

Xeno:
Seriously, man, I know you're afraid of squirrels but this is a little—

Selanio:
It wasn't funny! **(He lets go of Xeno and Brian, shoving them aside, and starts fiddling with the improbability generator.)** We'll see how you guys like it…

Brian:
D-don't touch that! You have no idea how it works!

Selanio:
Selanio understands that you put probability numbers in here and things happen, that's enough!

Ann:
But *anything* could happen, and it—

(Selanio hits the green button and there's a flash of light. When the light dies down, the machine is gone.)

Brian:
My… my machine! My beautiful… **(He starts hitting Selanio, but it doesn't really have any effect.)** You bastard!!

Selanio:
That's what you get. u_u

Ann:
Is everything else okay? What happened to the machine, I wonder?

(Brian, looking rather despondent, types into his computer the number he saw Selanio put in the machine. The computer analyzes it and…)

Brian:
Son of a… somehow, he managed to type in the exact probability of the entire machine just disappearing into thin air.

Ann:
Well, I suppose we should be grateful he didn't do anything worse.

Brian:
I'd only be grateful if he'd killed himself with it!

Xeno:
Selanio, what the fuck is your problem? Do you realize what you could have done?

Selan:
Or what you just did! Man, we could've fed that thing some tea and gotten ourselves an infinite improbability drive!

Selanio:
This is what happens when you turn people into squirrels. Squirrels are dangerous creatures, and of course a person will become dangerous after being one. u_u

Xeno:
This has nothing to do with you being a squirrel, Selanio, and everything to do with you being a *dick!*

Selan:
Selan is shocked you managed to type in such a comparatively harmless number though…

Selanio:
Who's to say it wasn't on purpose? Selanio is good at math, remember.

Brian:
Bullshit. It's completely impossible for you to have—

Selanio:
Impossible, or *improbable?*

(Selanio grins.)

Selan:
Impossible. u_u **(She starts pushing Selanio.)** Now let's go home. I have to come up with a suitable punishment for you.

(Selan and Selanio leave. Xeno scratches his head.)

Xeno:
Sorry, man. I had no idea he'd–

Brian:
Just go.

(Xeno leaves too. Brian leans back in his seat and sighs. He looks over at Ann.)

Brian:
I think you ought to know I'm feeling very depressed. -_-

-End: Episode forty-two.

043. Don't do it!

(It's Spring Break! Wooooo~! We find our villains at… Disney World? That's right! And who's this with them? It's Tavvy! Yep, Selan won four tickets to Disney in a contest and invited her three best friends to come with her. Right now they're walking away from their latest ride…)

Selanio:
Man, Selan, what's with you?

Selan:
Hm? What?

Selanio:
Those noises you were making on the ride!

Selan:
Everyone else was making noise too.

Selanio:
Everyone else was going "wooo" or screaming. You wouldn't stop squeaking like some anime character.

Selan:
Eeehh?

Tavvy:
I thought that was adorable. I couldn't stop laughing the whole ride, it was so amusing.

Xeno:
Yeah, it was pretty funny.

Selanio:
Selan can't be so adorable. It just isn't right.

Selan:
Why not? =<

Selanio:
You're supposed to be our fearless leader. Fearless leaders are not allowed to be adorable. u_u

Tavvy (chuckling):
Fearless leader? What?

Selan:
Selan is the *adorable* leader, thank you!

Xeno (smacking Selan and Selanio upside the head to remind them not to blow their cover):
Don't mind them, they're idiots.

Tavvy:
Okay… **(He looks around.)** Man, where is the bathroom?

Selan:
We passed it a while ago.

Xeno:
It's way back there.

Tavvy:
Oh. Damn. I'm just gonna run over there real quick, okay?

Selan:
'Kay.

(Tavvy runs off. Selanio notices something up ahead and runs over.)

Selanio:
It's the Sword in the Stone!

Selan:
It's… a photo-op thing!

Xeno:
What's the big deal?

Selanio:
Selanio heard that this is actually made so the sword can come out if you pull hard enough.

Xeno:
That sounds… dubious.

Selan:
Please don't try to pull the sword out.

Selanio:
Who said I was going to?

Xeno:
We know you. Don't do it.

Selanio:
Selanio was just going to pull a little. I wasn't going to use my whole strength.

Selan:
Don't do it!

Selanio:
Oh, calm down.

(He pulls on the sword… and promptly rips the entire sword, pedestal, and some of the floor it was attached to out of the ground. He drops it and looks around. Miraculously, no one saw anything—a show is going on nearby and everyone is looking at that instead. He backs away.)

Selanio:
Er…

Xeno:
Goddammit!

Selan:
… Let's go meet Tavvy at the bathrooms!

Selanio:

Good idea.

(They all run to the bathrooms. Xeno and Selanio sit down on a short wall outside the bathroom doors, and Selan decides to go into the girls' room.)

Xeno:

You're an idiot. You know that, right?

Selanio:

Shut up.

(Tavvy comes out of the bathroom.)

Tavvy:

Hey guys. Is Selan in the…?

Xeno:

Yeah.

Tavvy:

Okay.

(He sits down next to Selanio. There's a pause.)

Selanio:

So Selanio has noticed how you sit next to Selan on every ride.

Tavvy:

Hm? What?

Selanio:

Selanio knows this trick. It is so she clings to you when things get scary. u_u It's not very clever. -_O If you think it'll lead anywhere you are sorely mistaken.

(Selanio looms over Tavvy. Tavvy swallows a lump in his throat.)

Tavvy:

I wasn't… um… You know, I'm just gonna sit over here.

(Tavvy gets up, walks a few steps away to where Xeno is and sits by him.)

Tavvy (whispering):
Selanio is *terrifying.*

Xeno:
He is not.

Tavvy:
He's six-foot-six and looks at me like he's going to rip out my throat at any minute. O_o

Xeno:
Jeez, man, calm down. -_-

Selanio:
-_-; Selanio is annoyed when people talk like he isn't here, so I'll just go get an ice cream.

Xeno:
Go on, then.

(Selanio rolls his eyes and walks off.)

Xeno:
… Anyway. No, Selanio's been a bit off today. I think he's pissed at you.

Tavvy:
Why? Because I'm hanging out with Selan?

Xeno:
Maybe. Who knows. Sometimes he gets protective of her all out of nowhere. In his defense, though, you have been really clingy toward Selan. I saw you trying to hold her hand you know she's got this OCD thing about her hands, right? She's really picky about who she lets touch her hands, she'd have to really like you to—

Tavvy:
But she let Selanio hold her hand.

Xeno:
… What? When?

Tavvy:
Like three times already. Every time he sees something cool he grabs her hand and drags her to it.

Xeno:
That hardly counts, he's just dragging her around.

Tavvy:
She didn't seem to mind… **(He frowns.)** Do you think something's going on between—

Xeno:
No, never. Don't even talk like that, man, you're gonna make me sick.

Tavvy (getting a little worried):
You don't like Selan too, do you?

Xeno:
No, no. It's more like… you know how guys get pissed when they see their sisters going out with delinquents? It's like that.

Tavvy (relieved):
Oh. Okay.

Xeno:
But I'd like to think that she knows better than to get involved with someone like Selanio.

Tavvy:
Why do you even bother hanging out with him anyway? I mean, he's so… I dunno. Half the time he looks like he's about to don a cloak, laugh maniacally and try to take over the world.

Xeno (laughing):
Haaa, yeah. Well he's—he's annoying as hell, I'll give you that, and I can't rely on him for little things… but, you know… he's cool. Don't tell him I said this, but I'd trust him with my life. Not that he's ever given me *reason* to trust him, but… eh.

Tavvy:
…

(He looks away, trying to think if he has any friends he'd trust that much.)

Xeno:
And I definitely trust him to keep Selan out of trouble, provided he doesn't cause any trouble himself…

Tavvy:

Yeah… **(He looks over and sees Selanio marveling over some little thing. He decides to get off the heavy topic.)** … He's really enthusiastic about this place, huh?

Xeno (shrugging):

Yeah, well. There isn't a Disneyworld in Russia.

(Selan comes out of the bathroom)

Selan:

Hey homies! … Where'd Selanio go?

(Xeno points. Selan looks over, and squeals.)

Selan:

Oh em gee! Ice cream!

(Selan runs over to get some ice cream.)

Xeno:

… She's pretty easily amused, too.

Tavvy:

Yeah…

(Scene change! It's later in the day. They're at the exit now.)

Tavvy:

I'm still curious about whatever happened to the Sword in the Stone thing.

Selanio (apathetic):

It's a mystery. Jeez, the monorail just left, now we have to wait!

Xeno:

We could just ride the boats, you know.

Selan:

Boats are lame! Monorails are the wave of the FUTURE.

Xeno:

But those things were built decades ago.

Selan:

Wave of the FUTURE, Xeno!

Selanio:

The *FUTURE.*

Xeno:

We rode the monorail on the way here, can't we ride the boats?

Selanio:

Go ride them yourself. No one's stopping you.

Xeno:

Fine, I will. u_u **(He looks at Tavvy.)** And I assume you'll be going with Selan, then?

(Tavvy looks at Selan, then Selanio, then back at Selan.)

Tavvy:

You know, actually, I kinda wanted to ride the boat too.

Selan:

You two have fun on your lame, stuck-in-the-past BOATS. Come on, Selanio, race you to the FUTURE.

Selanio:

You're on!

(Selan and Selanio run off, racing each other up the stairs to the monorail station. Xeno looks at Tavvy incredulously.)

Xeno:

You aren't clinging to Selan. Are you sick?

Tavvy:

Hm? No, I just wanted to ride the boat.

Xeno:

Really.

Tavvy:

n_n;; R-really.

Xeno:

… all right, whatever. Come on, tiny, before the boat leaves.

(The two run to catch the next boat. As their boat departs, Tavvy leans against the rail and watches as the monorail

goes by. He sighs, smiles weakly, and waves as it zooms past.)

-End: Episode forty-three.

044. Read some comics!

(It's a fine day for evil! … or, rather, it was, until Apogee came and messed things up again. Now our villains are running away. They duck into an alley to catch their breath.)

Lady Ira:
Ugh… okay, I think it's time to change clothes.

Omen:
Agreed. Let's just—

(Suddenly, they hear a noise and look over—a shadowy figure has appeared in the alley. The three take fighting stances.)

Baron von Boom:
Hey! You'd better get out of here!

Lady Ira:
Yeah! We're three scary villains and we're in a foul mood!

???:
Oh, really.

(The figure walks out of the shadows.)

Omen:
… *Reza?*

Lady Ira:
Ehh? That guy who beat up the heroes a couple weeks ago?

Reza:
That would be me, yes.

Baron von Boom:
Let Baron von Boom shake your hand. u_u **(He walks over and shakes Reza's hand.)** You may have failed to kill the president, but anyone who can hospitalize a hero is awesome in my book.

Omen:
Er…

Reza:
I would like to speak with you three. Perhaps we can have a drink?

Baron von Boom:
Of course! Right, guys?

(Baron von Boom glares at the others.)

Lady Ira:
Ira has never done anything but mischief while in costume…

Baron von Boom:
Could be funny, people seeing us having a drink like normal peoplc. Hch.

Lady Ira:
Point. Arrite, let's do it.

(The three plus Reza all go to the nearest bar. Soon enough, they're all sitting at the counter—the men are all having beers while Selan drinks a coke. The area all around them is deserted, as everyone else in the bar has either left, or is cowering in the far corner, watching the villains carefully. A few people are taking pictures with their cell phones—it's not every day you see dangerous villains drinking and having

a civil conversation together in a public place.)

Reza (finishing telling about his last encounter with the superheroes):
It's a shame I was unable to win, but I suppose I got my message across. **(He chuckles.)** The authorities seem rather scared, knowing that I've returned.

Lady Ira:
I'll say! I bet Apogee's shaking in his boots.

Reza:
I'm sure he is. But enough about me. Miss Ira, tell me about yourself.

Lady Ira:
Eh? I dunno, what is there to tell?

Baron von Boom:
Yeah, all there is to Ira is bubbles and bossyness. u_u

Lady Ira:
Hey, shut up!

Baron von Boom:
See?

Lady Ira:
There's lots to me! I—I draw pictures, for one. u_u

Reza:
What do you draw?

Lady Ira:
Cartoons, you know…

Reza:
That's very interesting. n_n And you, Baron. I understand that you're from Russia?

Lady Ira:
As if his accent wasn't answer enough.

Baron von Boom (blatantly ignoring Ira):
Da, I am. u_u

Reza:

I've been to Russia a few times, you know.

Baron von Boom:

Pravda? Ti ponimayesh russkiy yazik?

Reza:

Ahaha. I actually had an interpreter with me whenever I went, so I never picked up the language.

Baron von Boom:

That's lame.

Reza:

Perhaps… **(He looks at Omen.)** You've been awfully quiet.

Baron von Boom:

He's always quiet. u_u

Omen:

I wish you'd do the same. -_O

Reza:

Is something the matter? You've barely even touched your drink.

Omen:

I'm just waiting for you to get to the point. I doubt you brought us here to make small talk.

Reza:

You're rather blunt, aren't you?

Omen:

Not to be impolite.

Reza:

Of course, of course. I'll just cut to the chase. As you all know, I've returned to the public eye, and as I'm sure you can guess I'm ready to begin my plans.

Omen:

What sorts of plans?

Baron von Boom:

World domination, I'd assume.

Reza:

Something like that. More like… just trying to change the world, as it were. But as powerful as I am, I can't do such a thing alone.

Omen:

So you need followers.

Reza:

Yes. But it is so very hard to find people willing to work with me. Everyone is either afraid to go against heroes or is afraid of *me*, although I can't imagine why.

Lady Ira:

So… wait, are you asking us…?

Reza:

Would you be willing to join the fight?

(Ira, Omen and the Baron all look at each other. Ira looks back at Reza.)

Lady Ira:

We're gonna have to discuss it. One moment. **(She looks to Omen.)** Hook us up with some telepathy, Omen.

(Omen nods, then touches a finger to both Ira and the Baron's foreheads.)

Omen (telepathically):

Testing, one, two…

Baron von Boom (also telepathically):

This isn't a microphone.

Lady Ira (also also telepathically):

Dudes, we can't agree to this thing.

Omen (… you get the idea):

Obviously.

Baron von Boom:

Selanio may admire his skills, but not enough to give up world domination.

Lady Ira:

Not to mention, working with him is like a death sentence if he wins!

Omen:

How so?

Lady Ira:

Dude, read some comics! Guys like him, they hire lackeys like us, then as soon as they're done with their plans they kill their lackeys to eliminate future threats! And also to avoid paying them.

Baron von Boom:

As stupid as the comic book comparison is, Selan's right. This guy's type tend to kill their subordinates once they've gotten a certain amount of use out of them.

Omen:

All right, so we definitely say no. But we gotta be careful not to piss him off. This guy's really powerful.

Lady Ira:

Let Selan handle this, I'm good at this sort of thing.

(Omen nods, and takes his fingers off his comrades' foreheads.)

Reza:

Hm? Well?

Lady Ira:

Well, the thing is, we've always been just the three of us, and we're just not comfortable joining a larger group.

Reza:

…

Lady Ira:

I mean, we admire your work, we do! It's great that you're trying to do so much for superpowered people's rights. We definitely won't stand in your way. It's just that we don't think we'd be comfortable being part of your army.

Reza:

I see. Well, I suppose I can't force you.

Lady Ira:

Nope. I-I mean, we're sorry.

Reza:
It's quite all right. Here, let's have another round of drinks, on me.

Lady Ira:
Thanks for being such a good sport. ^_^;

Omen (poking Baron von Boom's head to speak telepathically):
I have a bad feeling.

Baron von Boom:
Me too.

(Reza orders them all more drinks, they stick around and make more small talk, and then the villains part ways. Ira, the Baron and Omen, however, wonder if they haven't seen the last of Reza…)

-End: Episode forty-four.

045. I have super powers.

(The scene is the college! Tavvy and Cath are walking from their last classes. They decide to get a soda—they stop at the vending machines. A girl is standing in front of the one glass-cased one, glaring at it.)

Tavvy:
Ummm… Did the machine eat your money, or…?

Girl:
I hate these glass machines. >_<

Cath:
Okay…

Girl:
They make me feel useless.

Cath:
Riiiight… I'm just gonna…

(He puts some money in a nearby machine. He starts to press the 'Sprite' button…)

Girl:

Wait! Don’t press that button, it’s not Sprite!

Cath:

Sure.

(Cath presses the Sprite button. A Vault comes out. He glares at the girl.)

Girl:

I warned you.

Tavvy:

Did it rip you off too?

Girl:

No. u_u I have *super powers.*

Cath (drinking the Vault anyway):

Really.

Girl:

Yeah. I’m psychic! But my powers only work on vending machines.

Tavvy:

So you can see what’s in them?

Girl:

Yeah. See, Vault comes out when you press Sprite, Fanta comes out when you press Vault, Coke comes out when you press Root Beer, and Root Beer comes out when you press Coke.

Cath:

So where’s the Sprite?

Girl:

The Sprite is a lie.

Cath:

Jeez…

Girl:

Anyway, I’m Danni. You two are…?

Cath:

I’m Cath, and this here’s Mister Awkward McShypants.

Tavvy:
My name's not Awkward McShypa—

Cath:
Yes it is.

Danni:
Nice to meet you two. **(She shakes Cath's hand.)** Cath, and- **(She shakes Tavvy's hand, giggling.)** Mister McShypants.

Tavvy:
Er—I'm not—

Cath (seeing an opportunity for Tavvy to hang out with a girl who isn't Selan):
So, Danni, we were just thinking about getting something to eat. You wanna join?

Danni:
No, I'm anorexic. u_u

Tavvy:
Err…

Danni:
Kidding! I'm starved, let's go.

(Not long after, the three are at the cafeteria, all eating school food of questionable quality. Danni's telling them all about her job as a tech support technician.)

Danni:
So then this guy—he says—A? What's that?

Tavvy:
He didn't know what A was?

Danni (nodding):
And I say to him, it's a letter, you know, A! It's on your keyboard next to S.

Cath:
Then what?

Danni:
Duh. u_u; Then he asked me what an S was.

(They laugh.)

Cath:

… but seriously, though, you're laughing now but I'm sure that you wanted to wring his neck at the time.

Danni:

Thaaaaat's right. **(She drinks some soda.)** I swear this job's gonna give me an ulcer.

Tavvy:

Well, the pay's good at least, isn't it?

Danni:

Absolutely fantastic. But you have no idea how many times I've had someone ask for someone 'more qualified' to deal with as soon as they hear my voice. Half the time I have to pretend to just be a guy. "No, sir, my name's Jim, I just have a problem with my voice."

Cath:

I'm sorry, I wouldn't fall for that for a second.

Tavvy:

Me either.

Danni:

Well, you're in the minority, then. **(Siiip.)** But anyway, I've got a class to get to. I'll talk to you guys later, arrite?

Cath:

Okay.

Tavvy:

Have fun.

Danni:

See you~

(She gets up and leaves.)

Cath (after waiting for her to leave hearing range):

… Hot *damn.*

Tavvy:

Hm?

Cath:

You need to tap that.

Tavvy:
What?

Cath:
Look at her. She's totally hot and you're totally single. Go for it.

Tavvy:
But—But I—

Cath:
Don't tell me you're still hung up on Selan.

Tavvy:
Er…

Cath:
Listen. Danni's hot, she's funny, and she's smart. I'm pretty sure those are your requirements, right? And she's not an artist, sure, but she *is* a Comp. Sci. major, and that's pretty cool too.

Tavvy:
I-I guess…

Cath:
And… well, try and imagine this, okay? Picture this in your mind. Danni. Putting together a computer. *Completely naked.*

Tavvy:
Why is she naked?

Cath:
To prevent static discharge, obviously.

Tavvy:
Couldn't she just wear those wristbands, or ground herself or—

Cath:
That's not hot, Tavvy! Try and keep up, here!

Tavvy (getting miffed):
If she's so hot, why are you so eager for me to go out with her? Why don't you ask her out yourself?

Cath:

Because you're desperate and I'm not, obviously.

Tavvy:

It's not like you have a girlfriend!

Cath:

No, but I could. See, Tavvy, I know a hot girl when I see one. And I know how to talk to girls. I have no problem asking a girl out, and if she says no, well then I have no problem with that either. Unlike you—Mr. Awkward McShypants, gets so upset at the slightest rejection.

Tavvy:

Jeez…

Cath:

I'm just saying, you should ask Danni out. She seems like your type, and she doesn't seem to mind how quiet and shy you just were. That's a good sign.

Tavvy:

I-I know, it's just…

Cath:

Just what?

Tavvy:

I don't think I'm ready to ask anyone else out. Not yet.

Cath:

Fuck all this waiting around and trying to be ready. If you keep waiting to be ready for things, life's just gonna pass you by.

Tavvy:

…

Cath (standing up):

Fine, be hopeless. But I can't promise that I won't make a move on Danni, because *damn*. Anyway, I have to go to work.

Tavvy:

Okay.

Cath:

See you around. **(He starts to walk off.)** Jeez, you can save the world a hundred times but when it comes to girls…

Tavvy:

Eh? What?

Cath:

Nevermind. See you.

(Cath leaves. Tavvy sits there for a while more, picking at his food, pouting.)

-End: Episode forty-five.

046. Bye food!

(It's early afternoon, and Cath is on the phone with his cousin Tynan. The screen is split to see both of them; Cath is sitting on a bench somewhere on campus, and Tynan's sitting on his couch at home.)

Tynan:
So, hey, Cath.

Cath:
Yeah?

Tynan:
I was wondering if you had anything you wanted to say to me.

Cath:
Hm?

Tynan:
About Apogee, you know.

Cath:
Why would I have anything to say about him?

Tynan:
I think you know.

Cath:
I think you're paranoid.

Tynan:
I get this distinct feeling that you know his secret identity.

Cath:
Why would I know that?

Tynan:
Because I know you. Because I know the business you're in.

Cath:
Used to be in.

Tynan:
Whatever. Just fess up.

Cath:
I have nothing to fess up.

Tynan:
…

Cath:
…

Tynan:
… ugh.

Cath:
Gotta go?

Tynan:
Goddamn villains.

Cath:
Go kick some ass.

Tynan:
We'll talk later.

Cath:

I'm sure we will.

(Tynan and Cath hang up. Tynan glares at his phone.)

Tynan:

Dammit, Cath, you *know*. And I know you know.

(Later!! It's about an hour later and Tavvy and Cath are having lunch at the cafeteria. Cath, however, is in the bathroom. Tavvy's phone rings.)

Tavvy (answering the phone):

Hey, Tynan!

Tynan:

Hey, man.

Tavvy:

You okay?

Tynan:

A little out of breath. Just finished fighting off some villains.

Tavvy:

Ah. Arrest anyone?

Tynan:

Nah. Anyway, is Cath nearby?

Tavvy:

Hm? Nah, I mean, he's in the bathroom right now. Do you want to talk to him, or—

Tynan:

No, I just wanted to—agh… how do I put this?

Tavvy:

Huh?

Tynan:

Uh… here. You know, when we were kids, Cath used to do all this shit to annoy me, right?

Tavvy:

Yeah?

Tynan:

And one thing he always did was he'd stick spoons to me. Whenever I got upset I'd grow a magnetic field, so he'd just start sticking metal things to me, like spoons.

Tavvy:

Okay.

Tynan:

Can you do me a favor?

Tavvy:

Yeah?

Tynan:

Next time he gets upset or annoyed or something, stick a spoon or something to him.

Tavvy:

What? But that won't—

Tynan:

Just do it, okay? Anyway, I gotta go.

Tavvy:

Okay… Bye.

Tynan:

Bye. And remember—spoons!

(Tynan hangs up and Tavvy puts his phone away. Cath walks back from the toilets, looking pissed.)

Cath:

Goddamn, can't these people keep the bathrooms clean? God! A guy can't take a BM without fear of getting herpes or something from these filthy seats!

Tavvy:

…

(Tavvy picks up a spoon, looking unsure.)

Cath:

And of course, where's the toilet paper? I ask you! Where?!

**(Tavvy leans forward and sticks a spoon to Cathal's back. It

stays there.)

Cath:

… >_O… Tavvy.

Tavvy:

Yes?

Cath:

Have you been speaking with my cousin?

Tavvy:

Well…

Cath:

You know I really don't appreciate having spoons stuck to me.

Tavvy (picking up another spoon):

But how do they- **(he sticks on another one)** - stay? I mean, you're not magnetic like—

(Cath narrows his eyes, looking down at Tavvy.)

Tavvy:

… You *are.*

Cath:

I'm going to kill Tynan for this. >_<

Tavvy:

But you never told me you—

Cath:

Well, damn, now we've got to go have a private conversation. We gotta leave here and not eat our food. Bye food! Hope you're happy, you've just wasted one of your meals for the week.

(He grabs Tavvy by the arm and drags him out of the cafeteria.)

Tavvy:

But—but—since when have you been able to-

Cath:

Since always, man! I was born with it!

Tavvy:
You never told me!

Cath:
Gee, I wonder why! **(They get into a public bathroom that's empty. Cath locks the door so no one can walk in on their conversation.)** Maybe the same reason you never told me about your powers?

Tavvy (suddenly feeling very small):
You—you know I'm-?

(Cath just crosses his arms, looking very annoyed.)

Tavvy:
… **(He looks around, awkward.)** … there—there's—

Cath:
There's still a spoon on my back, isn't there.

Tavvy:
Two of them.

Cath:
Goddammit… **(He tries to reach to get them off.)**

Tavvy:
How long have you known?

Cath (still trying to reach the spoons):
A while. You know.

Tavvy:
How'd you figure it out?

Cath (finally managing to pull off a spoon):
Skillz.

Tavvy:
Oh. **(He pauses for a moment.)** But—but—this is great, Cath!

Cath (pulling on the second spoon—it won't come off):
Yeah? How so?

Tavvy:
Do you realize how much I need a sidekick, man? **(He gets all excited.)** We can be partners! Best friends, fighting

crime together!

Cath (pulling the spoon off and glaring at it):
No.

Tavvy:
What? Why?

Cath:
Like I really want to be a hermit like you. No thanks.

Tavvy:
But—but—

Cath:
Look, you might be cut out for the superhero thing, but I'm not.

Tavvy:
But you could be so great! I mean, Tynan's an awesome hero and you—

Cath:
I'm not him.

Tavvy:
But… you've got the same powers, don't you?

Cath (making sparks on his fingertips, just to demonstrate):
Pretty much.

Tavvy:
So why not?

Cath:
Too much of a bother.

Tavvy:
It's… it's fun sometimes.

Cath:
Oh, I don't doubt that.

Tavvy:
And… and if you don't want to deal with the Professor you don't have—Ah! The Professor! Do you know—

Cath:

Once I figured out your identity, it wasn't hard to figure out his.

Tavvy:

Oh.

Cath:

Look, I can't do this, alright? It's just not my thing.

Tavvy:

…

Cath:

If you ever need me, *really* need me, then sure, I'll come bail you out. But I'm talking life-or-death situations here. Any less and I'm not going to bother.

Tavvy:

… okay.

Cath:

Okay? **(He looks Tavvy in the eye.)** Man, you look like I just killed your mother.

Tavvy:

I do not. =<

Cath:

Okay, then you look like I just burned down your village.

Tavvy:

Stop with the similes. =<

Cath:

Whatever. Don't look so down, man. I guess—well, I guess now you've got someone else to come complain at when things get rough, right? Someone besides the Professor or Tynan.

Tavvy:

I guess.

Cath:

So buck up. **(He unlocks the door and opens it.)** Come on, let's go off-campus for lunch. The cafeteria sucked today anyway.

Tavvy:
All right…

-End: Episode forty-six.

Cath (on the phone with Tynan):
I'm going to *kill* you.

Tynan:
Hahaha~

Cath:
You have no idea how serious I am. >_<

047. Ya znayu.

(It's a weekday at the college! Selan's coming out of one of her classes, looking at her watch. She's supposed to meet up with Selanio soon for lunch! But suddenly, who comes along but—GASP—Stesha Zitomira!)

Stesha:
n_n Hey there.

Selan (has, by now, heard all Selanio's stories about this guy):
Uh, hey.

Stesha:
Funny running into you here, hm?

Selan:
Yeah, I'm sure >_>;;

(She starts looking around for Selanio.)

Stesha:
So, are you done with classes for the day?

Selan:
Eh? Well, yeah, but—

Stesha:
Do you want to go get lunch?

Selan:
What, with you?

Stesha:
Yes.

Selan:
Unn… chotto…

(Stesha opens his mouth to speak, but stops when someone behind him grabs him by the throat. And, of course, that someone is none other than Selanio, who does not look happy.)

Selan:
Oh look, it's Selanio~

Selanio (growling at Stesha):
Selanio seems to recall telling Zitomira to stay away from Selan. Tell me, am I imagining things?

Stesha:
Er…

Selanio:
In fact, Selanio recalls threatening to beat Zitomira into a bloody pulp, were he to make moves on Selan.

Selan:
Seriously?

Stesha:
I was just—

Selanio:
No excuses!

(Selanio starts dragging Stesha away. Selan follows.)

Selan:
Wait, you're not seriously going to—

Selanio:
Selanio is a man of his word!

Stesha:
Calm down, mate! I wasn't trying to—

Selanio:
Selanio knows your lies! I've heard them all a million times before!

(They get to a nearby alley, and Selanio throws Stesha into some trashcans. He rolls up his sleeves. Selan leans over to him.)

Selan (whispering):
Go easy. You could kill this guy easy and we don't want to deal with that sort of trouble.

Selanio (nodding):
Da, da, ya znayu.

Stesha (getting to his feet):
H-hey! I'm warning you, you shouldn't mess with me!

Selanio:
Oh, I'm so scared.

Stesha:
I mean it! I've got superpowers, you see!

Selanio (laughing):
Do you? Well, let's see them!

Selan:
Eh, maybe you shouldn't be so cocky…?

Stesha:
I'll use them! I will!

Selanio:
Go on!

(Stesha looks over Selanio, looking really nervous. He sizes Selanio up, then glances over at Selan—

and promptly shoots her with a laser out of his right eye.

The laser comes unexpectedly, and she's unable to block.

The beam goes straight through her chest. She falls back, and Selanio watches in horror as she hits the asphalt. He runs to her, and as he's distracted, Stesha books it out of there. Selanio takes Selan into his arms.)

Selanio:
Shit! Shit! Selan!

Selan:
Ffffuck…

Selanio:
Are you okay?

Selan:
Man, that hurt. **(She glances down the collar of her shirt to look at her chest.)** I don't think he damaged anything though…

Selanio:
That bastard!

(He drops Selan.)

Selan:
Ow! Hey, just cause I'm not dying doesn't mean you should be so rough…

Selanio:
Where the hell did he go?!

(He runs around, trying to find Stesha.)

Selan:
I mean, it still hurt, falling like that. Man, that had a lot of knockback…

Selanio:
Ugh! Of course, the bastard must be a master at running! **(He walks back over to Selan.)** Get up, lazy. Selanio still wants to get lunch.

Selan:
=< Man, where'd all the concern go?

Selanio:
Stop whining, baby whiner. Come on.

(Selanio starts walking off. Selan groans, pulling herself to her feet, and follows after Selanio.)

Selan:
So what was all this, Selanio trying to defend my honor?

Selanio:
It has nothing to do with your honor. u_u Selanio just hates Stesha fucking with the people he hangs out with is all.

Selan:
Really. Because it certainly sounded like you were trying to defend my honor.

Selanio:
Don't flatter yourself.

Selan:
And you looked so scared when you thought I was hurt! =< I don't think I've ever seen you look so scared.

Selanio:
Again, don't flatter yourself. u_u You were seeing things.

Selan (laughing):
Sure, sure. =D Well, since you got me shot, you have to pay for lunch.

Selanio:
Shto? Who says?!

Selan:
I do, stupid. u_u Now come on. Let's go off campus.

Selanio:
Godsdamn…

-End: Episode forty-seven.

Stesha (hiding in a janitor closet, on the phone with his dad):
Er… dad… could you come pick me up?

Annick (through the phone):
Let me guess. You picked a fight with someone bigger than you again.

Stesha:
Eh, well…

Annick:
I'm not picking you up. Also, you're grounded.

Stesha:
But—but dad!!

048. Kind of weird...

(It's an evening, and the scene is Xeno's store. Xeno's sitting at the cash register, looking bored as he lazily watches Gale stock shelves. He jumps a little when he hears the bell on the door ring, and he looks over to the door. Tavvy's there.)

Xeno:
Hey, it's you.

Tavvy:
Hn? Oh, Mister Reden. n_n;; I didn't know you worked here.

Xeno:
Yeah. And don't call me that, man, it makes me feel old.

Tavvy:
Sorry.

Xeno:
Anyway, what're you here for?

Tavvy:
Well, I was looking for some books on aliens… I needed to research something for an assignment, but the library mixes them all in with weird new-age stuff so…

Xeno:
Ah. Well, we've got that weird new-age stuff too, but we at least know to keep it on a separate shelf. Come on, follow me.

(Xeno leads Tavvy to a shelf and starts looking over the books. He pulls out one.)

Xeno:
This is a good book for beginners… what sort of thing were you needing, specifically?

Tavvy:
I mostly need descriptions and drawings of aliens… preferably from abductees.

Xeno:
Alright… **(He looks around, then pulls a few books down.)** Here. These should be all you need.

Tavvy (flipping through them):
Have you read all these already?

Xeno:
I've read pretty much everything on this shelf.

Tavvy:
Seriously?

Xeno (nodding):
And then some.

Tavvy:
I didn't think you were the type to be into this paranormal stuff…

Xeno:
To tell you the truth, kid, **(he reaches to a box on top of the shelf, grabs some books, and shoves them onto the shelf to replace the books he's taken out)** I'm actually trained as a paranormal investigator. I've got a BA in Mythology with focus in paranormal studies.

Tavvy:
Seriously? Then why are you… you know.

Xeno:
Working here?

Tavvy:
Yeah.

Xeno:
Life got in the way. I had bills to pay and no one else was hiring me.

Tavvy:
Oh…

Xeno (shrugging):
But whatever. That's just how things go. Do you need anything else?

Tavvy:
I don't know… is there anything you think I should…

Xeno (grabbing a plush doll off a nearby shelf):
Here, these are on sale.

Tavvy:
What is it?

Xeno:
It's a yellow alien doll. We're trying to get rid of them 'cuz they're not nearly as popular as the Mothman ones.

Tavvy:
It's kind of weird-looking…

Xeno:
Tell me about it. -_-; We can't get rid of these things.

(Xeno puts the doll back.)

Tavvy:
I guess I'll just buy these then.

Gale (from down the aisle):
Xeno! Get him to buy the spray!

Xeno:
Oh, right. We've got alien-away aerosol spray. u_u

Tavvy:
Now you're just trying to pawn off all your unpopular things on me. =<

Xeno:
Damn right.

Tavvy:
-_- Can I just pay?

Xeno:
Yeah, yeah. Come on.

(He leads Tavvy back to the cash register and starts ringing up his books.)

Tavvy:
So… if you're a paranormal investigator… have you ever seen an alien?

Xeno:
I'm not a paranormal investigator. I just *wanted* to be.

Tavvy:
R-right. Sorry. But still, have you ever…?

Xeno (looking away, thinking about what he should say):
No.

Tavvy:
I have.

Xeno:
Really.

Tavvy:
I got abducted once!

Xeno (not believing him):
Yeah? What happened?

Tavvy:
n_n;; … I don't really remember.

Xeno:
Then how do you know you got abducted?

Tavvy (laughing—he can't just tell Xeno that the aliens gave him superpowers, after all):
Ahaha… I guess it's kind of stupid, huh.

Xeno (keeping in mind that he can't remember much of his abduction, either):
Nah, it's not that dumb… but you'll make yourself look crazy, telling everyone stuff like that.

Gale (walking up and putting an empty box on the counter):
Obviously he's crazy. Look at the hair.

Tavvy:
I—I like my hair…

Gale:
How much money do you waste on hair dye, man?

Tavvy:
It's worth it, I like having green hair…

Xeno (smacking Gale on the head):
Leave him alone, jackass, he's a customer.

Gale:
Whatever. Do you know where Dougal left the shipment of meditation books?

Xeno:
Probably in the back of the stock room, genius.

Gale (walking off):
Right, right…

Xeno:
Anyway. Did you ever report your abduction to anywhere?

Tavvy:
n_n;; No, no…

Xeno:
If you got hypnotism therapy you might be able to figure out what happened. Just as long as you don't go to a quack.

Tavvy:
Well, I don't…

Xeno:
I know a guy. I mean, he was one of my teachers in college, he seemed like he knew what he was doing…

Tavvy:
It's okay. I'm probably better off not knowing.

Xeno (shrugging):
Yeah, probably. Anyway, all this'll be forty-one fifty.

(Tavvy hands over his credit card. Xeno swipes it, hands it back, puts the books in a bag and gives them to Tavvy.)

Xeno:
There you go. Have fun.

Tavvy:
Thanks. n_n;; I'll see you around.

Xeno:
Yeah, see you.

(Tavvy leaves. Gale returns, carrying a box.)

Gale:
So I thought you said you were abducted, too.

Xeno:
I never said that. u_u

Gale:
You're a liar. -_O

Xeno:
Yeah, maybe I am. Now go stock those books, else I'll tell Dougal how rude you were to the customer.

Gale:
Jeez…

(Gale takes the box and wanders off.)

-End: Episode forty-eight.

049. I don't get it!

(It's the weekend at Selan et al.'s house, and Xeno's hanging out in his room, using his computer, when Selanio comes in.)

Selanio:
Hey, man, wanna go clubbing or something?

Xeno:
Hm? Why?

Selanio:
Because I've noticed something.

Xeno:
What's that?

Selanio:
You spend too much time around here. -_O

Xeno:
Huh?

Selanio:
If you're not at work or hanging out with us, you're

here. In your room or watching TV. It's lame. You need to stop being a hermit and go live a little. So get off your ass, we're hitting the bars.

Xeno:
Don't you have studying to do this weekend?

Selanio:
I'll do it tomorrow. Come on.

(Later that night! They're sitting at a bar, drinking. Selanio looks like he's having a pretty good time, but Xeno looks pretty miserable.)

Selanio:
Stop sulking.

Xeno:
I'm not sulking. -_-

Selanio:
Yes you are, loser, stop it.

Xeno:
I'm not. u_u; I'm just a little discouraged is all.

Selanio:
What, just 'cause that chick splashed her drink in your face?

Xeno:
Yes. -_O And the fact that you've gotten a number from every chick you've talked to and here I just talk to one and I get martini in my face!

Selanio:
She doesn't count, she was drunk.

Xeno:
Isn't that supposed to make things easier? >_<

Selanio:
Depends on the girl. **(He downs a shot and looks around.)** Here, look over there. Hot brunette at two o'clock.

Xeno:
Nope, she's gay.

Selanio:

Eh? How can you- **(Xeno gives him one of those "I'm psychic, idiot" looks, and Selanio shrugs.)** Right, right. Okay, try that girl with the black hair.

Xeno:

What the hell am I even supposed to say? I hate these places, I'd much rather meet a girl at some place where, I don't know, there's something worth talking about…

Selanio:

Like where?

Xeno:

Like… a museum? Or… or a store, I guess?

Selanio:

Museum? Pfft. Lame.

Xeno (groaning):

Can I just have one of the numbers you got? You're never gonna call them anyway.

Selanio:

Selanio will not be an accessory to false advertising. u_u

Xeno:

False advertising?

Selanio:

Yes. Girl gets call and expects to meet up with the hot Russian guy she gave her number to, but then finds herself on a date with ugly Indian guy. That's false advertising!

Xeno:

I'm not ugly. -_-;

Selanio:

Sure you are. Now go talk to that chick over there.

Xeno:

Ugh, I can't do it. >_< I'm not all suave and cool with chicks like you, man—although, honestly, why do girls even like you, man, you're a jerk.

Selanio:
Girls love jerks. Everyone knows this. Also I'm very good-looking and I have a sexy accent. u_u You should try talking with an accent.

Xeno:
I don't know how to talk with an accent.

Selanio:
Maybe you should try speaking other language?

Xeno:
My Hindi's terrible, though…

Selanio:
Doesn't matter. Sometimes when I talk to these girls I say things like, 'your nose hair needs trimming', but they still think it sounds sexy because they don't know what I'm saying. You just walk up and say something like, "Where I come from, we have a saying," and then you say anything really.

Xeno:
What do I say if they ask what that means?

Selanio:
Say it can't be translated, means nothing. They should laugh. Then you ask if you can buy them a drink.

Xeno:
Okay… I guess I'll try it.

(Xeno finishes off his beer, then walks over to the chick Selanio had pointed out earlier. He comes back a little while later, and motions for the bartender to give him another drink.)

Selanio:
Hm, didn't work?

Xeno:
She's a Hindi language major!

Selanio (laughing):
So you said something dumb?

Xeno:
Afterwards I apologized and told her it was all your

idea.

Selanio:
Da? And then?

Xeno (hissing, angry):
And then I made the mistake of pointing to you!

Selanio:
Why is this a mistake?

Xeno (pulling out a slip of paper):
This is why! **(He hands the paper over to Selanio.)** She… she wants you to call her sometime. -_-;

Selanio (laughing, putting the paper in his pocket):
Selanio is so very popular with the ladies.

Xeno:
Why?! I don't get it! You're annoying! You're self-absorbed!

Selanio:
Am not. **(He takes a drink.)**

(Xeno gets his new drink and chugs it down. He sits there silently for a moment.)

Xeno:
What do you do with all those, anyway? What's the point in asking all these girls for their numbers? I've seriously never seen you call one of them even once.

Selanio:
You want to know?

Xeno:
Why, is it something I wouldn't want to?

Selanio (shrugging):
Selanio keeps them in a book.

Xeno:
What for?

Selanio:
For amusement. See how many I can get.

Xeno:

That's awful.

Selanio:

Not really. Some guys keep tabs on how many girls they fuck. Selanio is a little classier, I just collect phone numbers. It's a book full of possibilities that never were. u_u

Xeno (narrowing his eyes and taking Selanio's drink away from him):

The time you start sounding poetic, Selanio, is the time you've had too much.

Selanio (taking his drink back):

No, you'll know when I'm too drunk when I stop speaking English.

Xeno (rolling his eyes):

And then you drop your pants. Now I remember. **(He sighs.)** Maybe it's for the best I'm so lousy with women though.

Selanio:

Hm, why? You gay?

Xeno:

No. >_O I was just saying, you know, I've never actually had a girlfriend since, you know… **(He pokes Selanio's forehead to use his telepathy so other people won't hear.)** *Since I got my powers. Since I have to work so hard to control my emotions, I don't really know how having a girlfriend would affect me.*

Selanio:

Don't be a wuss. You can't just decide to swear off women because you're too afraid of what might happen.

Xeno:

I can imagine things getting pretty bad!

Selanio:

This is because you're a pessimist.

Xeno:

No, I'm just realistic. -_-;

Selanio:

Lame. u_u;

Xeno (sighing):

Whatever. I don't even like the types of girls who come to these places anyway.

Selanio:

Eh, Selanio doesn't either.

Xeno:

Then why'd we even come here?

Selanio:

Because you're desperate. u_u

Xeno:

Fuck you! **(He fumes for a minute.)** Out of curiosity…

Selanio:

Yes?

Xeno:

What kind of girl DO you like, anyway? I can't seem to figure it out from the girls I've seen you date. -_O And actually, come to think of it, you're a lot like Selan. You rarely give anyone a second date…

Selanio:

Selanio likes not-easy girls.

Xeno:

Oh yeah? I find that hard to believe.

Selanio:

What, because girls throw themselves at Selanio, Selanio has to like the types of girls who throw themselves at guys?

Xeno:

I guess not, but…

Selanio:

Poslushaytye. Selanio's parents were very close, da? My mother was always there for my father. Through bad times as well as good. Selanio wants a woman like that. Do you really think these easy girls would be so dedicated?

Xeno:

Probably not.

Selanio:

If Selanio came home from a battle with his face all scarred, I'd end up quickly without a girlfriend. u_u Selanio is willing to work a little harder for a girl who doesn't care what Selanio looks like. Even if I am a sexy bitch.

Xeno:

See, you start sounding pretty respectable, then you blow it with your ego. 9_9

Selanio:

Well I am!

Xeno:

Whatever. -_-;

Selanio:

Now! Go hit on that redhead over there!

Xeno:

O_o;; I sense… that she's carrying a huge bottle of pepper spray in that purse.

Selanio:

So don't fuck up! **(He pushes Xeno toward the girl.)** Go! Go!

-End: Episode forty-nine.

Selan:

Man, Xeno, what happened to your eyes?!

Xeno:

Selanio's poor judgement. >_<

050. I approve!

(Chandra sits atop the roof of the tallest skyscraper. She stares at the sky, thinking about why she's there.)

(Two weeks ago…)

(Ann and Selan are hanging out at the library. Ann pulls out a piece of paper.)

Ann:
Selan, take a look at this.

Selan (eating a sandwich she snuck in):
Hn? Somefin' about an old villain?

Ann (nodding):
Brian's felt a little bad about not having powers lately, right? So I was doing research on other mad scientist villains, see if I could find anything to encourage him. But then I found this. It's Beta, an old villain from the Professor's day. When they arrested him they got his real name—look. **(She points.)**

Selan:
Joseph Pazzesco?

Ann:

That's Brian's last name. That's Brian's *dad,* Selan!

Selan:

Oooh.

Ann:

That's not all. I did a little more digging, tried to get a photo of Beta's partner, Gamma. Look. **(She shows a photo.)** I'm pretty certain that's Brian's mom.

Selan:

Ooh. The plot thickens. **(She takes another bite of her sandwich.)**

Ann:

I need to find out more about this…

Selan:

What's Brian say about it?

Ann:

I doubt he has any idea. I don't think he even knows who his father is. I don't want to bother him with it unless I know more.

Selan:

Well, good luck. Villain information is really top-secret. All that stuff on Wikipedia's just hearsay. Only government agents and heroes are given any reliable info.

Ann:

Hmm…

(One week ago…)

(The city is under attack! But the one attacking is… Chandra?! On her own, no less! She's dropping bombs on the streets, although it certainly looks like she's being as careful as she can to not actually harm anyone. Soon, Apogee shows up, looking a bit confused.)

Apogee:

Okay, where's Quantum?

Chandra:

On vacation.

Apogee:
Well, tell him that—

Chandra:
He didn't order me to do this, I swear.

Apogee:
Oh. **(He scratches his head.)** Are you okay? Not sick or anything?

Chandra:
-_-; This isn't like me at all, I know...

Apogee:
So... are we gonna fight, or...?

Chandra:
Actually, I—here. **(She hands him her remaining bombs.)** I actually just wanted to get your attention. Sorry. n_n;; It's just that it's not like you've got a number I can call...

Apogee (making sure the bombs are unlit):
Uh... okay?

Chandra:
It's just... I kind of wanted to have a word with the Professor. And I know you're the only person who really knows how to get in contact with him...

Apogee:
The Professor? Why?

Chandra:
It's really personal. Could you just, you know... tell him to meet me on top of the tallest building in town. Say... Friday at midnight?

Apogee:
O-okay...

Chandra:
Thanks! I'm counting on you. n_n

(Chandra flies off and Apogee is a bit too dumbfounded to chase after her. He just shakes his head and leaves.)

(Back to now...)

(Professor Pain lands on the roof. Chandra stands, smiling politely at the retired superhero.)

Chandra:
I'm sorry to inconvenience you.

Professor Pain:
Normally I don't do this sort of thing.

Chandra:
I know.

Professor Pain:
I'm only here because I know you aren't the type to set a trap.

Chandra:
Thank you.

Professor Pain:
Now what do you want? I've things to attend to.

Chandra:
O-of course. Here. **(She hands him the paper with information on Beta.)** I've been doing research on other mad scientists, and this one caught my interest. I was wondering, since you caught him and all, if you know anything else about him?

Professor Pain:
Beta? Why, I don't suppose you know where Gamma might be hiding herself, would you?

Chandra:
n_n; No clue.

(The Professor looks Chandra over for a moment, trying to consider what harm she might do with the information. Eventually he sighs and hands the paper back to her.)

Professor Pain:
… he's being kept at the state mental hospital. Anything you need to know, ask him yourself.

Chandra:
Thank you.

Professor Pain:
And if you break him out, I'll know it was you.

Chandra:
I wouldn't dream of it. Thank you so much.

(The Professor shrugs and turns to leave. He stops.)

Professor Pain:
And goddammit, stop being so polite. I know you aren't very good at being evil but you could at least *try*.

Chandra:
Umm… Bwa ha ha?

(The Professor shakes his head and sighs, then fires his jetpack and disappears into the night sky.)

(It's a while later, and Ann is walking into the state mental hospital, signing all the forms and waivers that visitors are required to sign. Eventually she's led through the halls and the guard puts her in a guest room, where a red-haired man is sitting on the other side of a glass pane. Ann sits down and the guard leaves the room.)

Joseph:
It's not very often I get visitors. Oh, you're not from a church, are you? Which one? Because if you're one of those crazies I'm calling for the guard right now. =<

Ann:
No, no. n_n; I'm… I'm a friend of your son's.

Joseph:
My son? **(He sits up straight, attentive.)** You… oh! I see! You're his girlfriend, aren't you?

Ann (blushing):
Ah, well…

Joseph:
Oh, you're adorable! I approve! When's the wedding?

Ann:
n_n;; I think you might be getting a little ahead of yourself…

Joseph:
Although, you know, it's a bit odd, meeting my son's girlfriend before I meet my son…

Ann:
I know. ^^; Here, hold on for a moment…

(She pulls something out of her purse—it's disguised as a lipstick, but when she opens it it's some sort of antenna. She pushes a button.)

Joseph:
Ooh. What's that?

Ann:
I'm jamming any wire taps that might be in here. I'm sure the guards are trying to listen in on us.

Joseph:
Yeeeaaah, they do that. **(He yawns.)** You get that from Meredith?

Ann:
Hm? Brian's mom? Why, does she have one?

Joseph:
Prob'ly. She's got all kinds of that sort of thing. So you made that thing, then?

Ann:
Well, Brian helped…

Joseph:
So he inherited his mom's brains? Good, good. n_n; I can't say I'd want him turning out as dumb as me.

Ann:
Look, about Meredith…

Joseph:
I assume you probably know about her, right? I mean, if you're jamming up wire taps and stuff…

Ann:
Well, I assumed…

Joseph:
How's she doing? Not still robbing banks, is she?

Ann:

Not that I know of.

Joseph:

Oh, good. That woman tends to get herself in trouble. Now, about Brian…

Ann:

Y-yes…?

Joseph:

How is he? Does he look like me? How tall is he? He doesn't have my weird eyes, does he?

Ann (trying to keep up with the questions):

Er… he's fine, yes, about 5'4" and still growing, no but they're still green and he wears glasses.

Joseph:

Neat. So why'd you come to visit, anyway?

Ann:

Curiosity, I guess.

Joseph:

Why isn't Brian here?

Ann:

Well… I guess because he doesn't know you're here? I don't think Meredith's ever told him anything about you…

Joseph:

Oh. **(He pauses.)** I'd be sadder about that, but they've got me on all these pills to keep me happy.

Ann:

Oh…

Joseph:

But—but it's okay. I know, Meredith's just trying to keep Brian out of trouble. Wouldn't want him realizing his dad's a criminal, I see.

Ann:

But Meredith's…

Joseph:

But Brian doesn't *know* that, see. u_u; I'm sure

Meredith knows what she’s doing. She’s always got these things planned out.

Ann:
Okay… anyway, I was kind of curious about…

Joseph:
About the villainy thing? Oh man, it was so much fun. Mer would just give me all these cool lasers and we’d cause so much trouble.

Ann:
n_n Sounds fun. How did… you know…

Joseph:
How’d I end up here?

Ann:
Yeah.

Joseph:
Things just went wrong I guess. We—there was a big show at the museum, one of those traveling things? With all these huge gems. Mer wanted to steal them, but one of my lasers backfired and it hurt and then next thing I knew, the good Professor had me in cuffs… I thought Mer would come to break me out, I really hoped, but…

Ann:
I’m sorry.

Joseph:
It—it’s okay. See, see, I found out later—later, after the trial, I found out she was pregnant at the time. But even before I found out, I still was careful. I told them Meredith wasn’t Gamma, that I was having an affair with Gamma and that Meredith had nothing to do with anything. I can see why she didn’t rescue me. She couldn’t risk getting hurt, what with the baby and all. I see.

Ann (doesn't really think that's the reason at all):
Yes. I’m sure that’s it. n_n;; …Does- does Meredith ever come visit you?

Joseph:
No. n_n;; I haven’t seen her since they brought me here. I’m sure she doesn’t want to risk people finding out her secret identity. I mean, she has Brian to worry about

and all. Is she doing okay? I hope she's supporting herself without the crime to fall back on.

Ann:
She's doing fine. She's been taking good care of Brian. n_n

Joseph:
Good, good.

(A bell sounds, indicating that Ann's time with Joseph is up. She grabs the antenna and shoves it into her purse just before a guard comes in to escort her out.)

Joseph:
T-tell Brian to come visit me, okay? If it's possible. Please?

Ann:
Okay. Take care of yourself.

Joseph:
You too. Thanks.

(Ann leaves and is escorted out of the asylum. Ann stands outside for a while.)

Ann (Narration box): *From a technical standpoint, Meredith and Joseph—that is, Gamma and Beta—were nearly identical to Brian and I. They relied on technology to do their fighting in lieu of any actual superpowers and Joseph, like myself was, according to what I read, not particularly aggressive, mostly just following Meredith's orders and being friendly with law enforcement and the Professor.*
He was the Chandra to Meredith's Quantum.
But on a personal level, the similarities ended. If Meredith treated Joseph anything like she treats Brian, it's clear that the trust and caring that Brian and I share was entirely absent. If Joseph were to get hurt, I doubt Meredith would have flown into a rage like Brian does for me. And of course, Brian would never let me get locked up here. He'd rather die.

Joseph didn't belong here. It was Meredith's fault that he was stuck in this miserable place, but of course she couldn't be bothered to break him out.
… I had to do something.

(Scene change! It's night. There's no moon, and it's pitch black outside. Chandra, carried by her jetpack, flies from window to barred window, looking inside, until…
She stops. She pulls out a set of night-vision goggles, uses them to look inside the window and confirm that this is, in fact, Joseph's cell, and then rests the goggles atop her head. She pulls a device from her belt and places it upon the wall. Gingerly, she presses a few buttons, and then there's a shaking—and the wall crumbles down. An alarm goes off.)

(Joseph sits up in his bed, looking around confusedly. He notices Chandra floating outside the new hole in his wall.)

Joseph:
Who the—

Chandra:
I'm—I'm Chandra.

Joseph (watches the news):
Seriously? No you're not. I can tell your voice. You're—

Chandra:
Well, I—

Joseph:
… oh. Oh, I see.

Chandra:
Please, come with me.

Joseph:
So then, Quantum is…

Chandra:
Yes.

Joseph:
Can't say I'm surprised. Oh well.

Chandra:
Look, the guards'll be here any minute. Please, you have to get out of here!

Joseph:
Why?

Chandra:
Because—because you don’t belong here.

Joseph:
But I really do.

Chandra:
But—

Joseph:
Look, I did a bunch of bad stuff and I got caught, okay? It’s only fair that I stay here.

Chandra:
But it wasn’t your idea to do any of that! It wasn’t your fault!

Joseph:
I could’ve said no. I could’ve stopped at any time.

Chandra:
…

Joseph:
Just go. Please.

Chandra:
I’m sorry.

Joseph:
It’s okay.

Chandra:
I’ll leave.

Joseph:
Take care of Brian for me.

Chandra:
I will. Goodbye.

(Chandra flies away just as the guards run into the room, rather surprised to find Joseph still in it. She holds back tears as she flies away, hoping with all of her heart that she and Brian never end up like their predecessors.)

-End: Episode fifty.

051. No fair!

(It's a weekend, and Apogee and the Professor are at the Professor's top-secret training ground. Oddly enough, Cath's with them.)

Marika:
Come on, Tavarius, you can do better than this.

Apogee (out of breath):
But… but how am I supposed to dodge *lightning?!*

Cath:
Excuses, excuses. **(He shoots another bolt at Apogee, who gets hit by it.)** See, this is why you never arrest anyone.

Marika:
Seriously. **(He sighs.)** By the way, Cathal.

Cath:
Hm?

Marika (remembering the bank robbings from forever ago):
With those powers of yours, I don't suppose you're able to, say… make an electromagnetic pulse?

Cath (chuckling):
Course not. Why would I want to?

Marika:
Just asking.

Cath (throwing more lightning at Apogee):
C'mon, dodge already! How are you supposed to beat Reza like this?

Apogee:
Reza's blasts aren't nearly as fast as yours!

Cath:
Exactly! If you can dodge my blasts, then Reza should be cake!

(Cath and Apogee continue sparring. Cath laughs.)

Cath:
Heh, you're lucky I'm no villain, Tav. I'd have the city taken over in no time if I were.

Apogee:
Hey, you're only winning because I'm just defending, here!

Cath:
Sure. But I'm kicking your ass with lightning alone. Let's see how well you'd do in a city environment, when there's metal all over for me to throw at you.

(Cath tosses a lightning ball.)

Apogee (barely dodging):
Hey, can you do that thing Tynan does? With the metal disc and the flying and all?

Cath (frowning, charging up more lightning):
Tynan's a show-off.

Apogee:
So you can't?

Cath (tossing the lightning):
Shut up, man.

Marika:
Apogee. Try to apprehend him.

Cath:
Eh? Hey! I didn't agree to that!

Marika:
Well, if you aren't going to use your powers to help the city, you might as well be a better help to us.

Cath:
Ugh. Fine, fine, Professor Pain-in-the-ass.

Apogee:
Ready?

Cath:
Don't ask me if I'm ready! I'm supposed to be a villain, over here.

Apogee (laughing):
Right, right. Here I come!

(Apogee and Cath fight for a while. Eventually, Apogee knocks Cath down, and tries to put a pair of handcuffs on him—when Cath uses his magnetism powers to put the cuffs on Apogee instead. Cath laughs, getting back onto his feet.)

Cath:
I win.

Apogee:
No fair!

Cath:
Gotta be prepared for anything.

Apogee:
But none of the villains I fight have magnetic powers anyway, so they can't do that!

Cath:
Omen's telekinetic, he probably could if he tried.

Apogee:
But he wouldn't!

Cath:

Oh yeah? Why do you think that?

Apogee:

Because… **(He clumsily rummages through the pouch on his belt, looking for the handcuff key.)** Because he's got some good in him. I know it.

Cath:

So you think that for that reason, he'd choose to *not* use every chance he has to not get arrested? **(He shakes his head.)**

Apogee:

I just don't think he'd be as sneaky as that.

(Apogee gets the key out and hands it to Cath.)

Cath:

I think he would. No villain wants to get caught. Getting caught means potentially losing your secret identity. Losing your secret identity means having to abandon any life you've got going currently go either start a new one, or go fugitive. It's not a pleasant thought.

Apogee:

I—I guess.

Cath (unlocking the handcuffs):

Why do you say that of Omen, though, anyway? Him specifically, I mean.

Apogee:

Well, because… because Indrid chose him, you know? And Indrid is like… this guardian of Earth guy. If he's trying so hard to protect the planet, he wouldn't give those powers to someone completely evil.

Cath:

So? Big deal. Let me tell you something. It's not just Omen who's got a good side. You'd be hard-pressed to find *any* villain that's without their redeeming qualities. Even Reza's probably got some good in him. Pure evil's nearly impossible to find.

Apogee:

That's… a good thing to think about, I guess.

Cath:

No, it isn't. It means that just because someone's got some good in them, doesn't mean you can trust them or think that they'd ever want to toss aside their bad ways to join the forces of good or anything stupid like that. It just means that their bad side is loud enough to drown out their conscience. **(He looks at the Professor.)** Isn't that right, Professor?

Marika:

Yes. I'll admit to being just as trusting as Tavarius when I was his age. I've since learned, though, that you can't change a villain's ways. I've tried, it never worked.

Apogee:

That's… that's sad.

Marika:

It is. But it's true.

Cath:

That's just the way things work, kiddo. The way of the world, and all that.

Apogee:

…

Marika (looking at his watch):

I've got to go pick Audi up from school. You two, keep sparring until I get back.

Apogee:

Yes, sir.

(The Professor leaves. Cath sighs.)

Cath:

Man, you always gotta make those mopey faces at me.

Apogee:

I'm not—

Cath:

Yeah, you are. **(He rolls his eyes.)** Look, I'll tell you something to cheer you up, just don't tell the Professor anything about it.

Apogee:

Okay.

Cath:

Look, I used to be—well, I won't say I was a villain, but I was a *criminal*, okay? And now look at me, helping you out and all.

Apogee:

So people *can* change.

Cath:

Sure. But I wouldn't count on it, if I were you.

Apogee:

… so you were a criminal, huh? **(He snickers.)** What'd you do, steal candy bars?

Cath:

What, you think I'm kidding around here?

Apogee:

Yeah. C'mon, what'd you do??

Cath:

Ugh. Okay, you know all those bank robberies a while back? Remember when your jetpack got knocked out by an EMP?

Apogee:

You mean…

Cath (pointing to himself):

Yo.

Apogee:

But you just told Marika that you couldn't make an EMP!

Cath:

I *lied.*

Apogee:

Do you realize how much hell the Professor gave me for not catching you?

Cath (shrugging):

Hey, blame Harlan, he was the getaway guy. Either way, the money got returned to the banks, didn't it?

Apogee:
Well… yeah…

Cath:
So stop whining. Let's get back to sparring.

Apogee:
Okay… **(He takes a fighting stance.)** Does Tynan know you robbed banks?

Cath:
What's this obsession with Tynan? And yes. We're not so good at keeping secrets from each other. Both of us are sneaky *bastards.*

Apogee:
I dare not imagine what growing up with you two was like. =<

Cath:
It was awesome and involved huge amounts of blackmail. Incoming!

(Cath shoots lightning at Apogee.)

-End: Episode fifty-one.

052. Just checking.

(The scene is Brian's room. Brian had been writing in one of his school notebooks, but he's stopped, thanks to something Ann's said…)

Brian:
My father is-?!

Ann (nodding):
He's Beta. I—I met him. And your mother…

Brian:
Oh god. Don't tell me she's Gamma, Ann. Don't you dare tell me that.

Ann:
… um. All right. I won't tell you that.

(… pause …)

Brian:
Dammit. Just say it already.

Ann:
Your mother's Gamma.

Brian:
Goddammit!

Ann:
I thought you admired Gamma though. You based a lot of your inventions on her designs.

Brian:
But—but you don't understand, Ann! I might admire her but dammit that woman's *scary!* And you're telling me she's been *my mother* this whole time?! The woman who, this very moment, is sitting downstairs shredding the junk mail?!

Ann:
You know, despite knowing how it's like, it still feels odd thinking about villains doing mundane stuff like that…

Brian:
You're missing the point. Oh god, and here I thought I was afraid of her finding about about this *before*…

Ann:
Do you really think she would mind you being a villain?

Brian:
Are you kidding? Even drunks punish their kids for drinking!

Ann:
Good point…

Brian:
Ugh, now I *really* need to get an A in English…

Ann:
That's not even the most important part though. About your father…

Brian (resuming working on his homework):
Yeah, what about him?

Ann:
I think you should see him.

Brian:
Yeah, no thanks.

Ann:

Why not?

Brian:

I've gone this long without meeting him, I don't see why I should change that.

Ann:

He really wants to see you though.

Brian:

So? He can call and ask himself, can't he? They allow phone calls in jail.

Ann:

I think he's afraid to call here. He's afraid of incriminating Meredith.

Brian:

… or just afraid of Meredith, you mean.

Ann:

Perhaps.

Brian:

I don't want to see him.

Ann:

Brian, you have to. He—he needs to see you. He needs you.

Brian:

I don't care.

Ann:

How can you be so heartless?

Brian:

I'm not being heartless, I'm- **(He looks up at Ann.)** -you're going to cry, aren't you.

Ann:

I am not.

Brian:

Don't cry.

Ann:

I'm not going to…

Brian (hugging her):

Why the hell is this so important?

Ann:

You didn't see him. He was so sad.

Brian:

Well, *yeah*. He's in jail. That's not exactly candyland.

Ann:

Meredith abandoned him. She could have broken him out of there before they got his identity but she didn't, she just let him take the fall for her.

Brian:

Yeah, I wouldn't put that past her.

Ann:

… you… you wouldn't let that happen to me, would you?

Brian:

How could you even ask that?

Ann:

I—I don't know, I…

Brian (holding her closer):

Just because my mother's a bitch doesn't mean that I have to repeat her mistakes. You know I'd rather die than let anything happen to you.

Ann:

I know…

Brian:

You okay?

Ann:

Yeah.

Brian:

Come on, let's get back to work.

Ann (nodding):
Un. **(She opens her book.)** … so you're going to visit your father, right?

Brian:
No.

Ann (furrowing her brow):
Brian…

Brian:
Okay, I'll… think about it.

(Just then, Meredith opens the door and looks in.)

Meredith:
Brian?

Brian (terrified):
Ye—yes…?

Meredith:
Just making sure you're not doing anything unspeakable to that poor girl. -_O

Brian:
>_<…

Ann:
I'm fine, Mrs. Pazzesco.

Meredith:
Just checking.

(She leaves.)

(Brian sits silently, glaring at the door as he listens to Meredith walking down the hall and back downstairs.)

Brian:
… I still *hate* her.

Ann:
Seriously.

-End: Episode fifty-two.

053. Hn? Shto?

(It's evening in our villains' house. Xeno and Selanio are sitting on the couch watching some action movie when Selan rushes in and sits down between them, holding her laptop.)

Selan:
Guys! Guys!!

Selanio:
What? Can't you see we're trying to watch a movie?

Selan:
Huh? What movie?

Xeno:
I don't even know.

Selanio:
We didn't catch the title. But—look at that, things keep exploding. It's amazing!

Selan:
Neat. But—no, guys, look! Check this out! People are writing FANFICTION about us!

Xeno:

What?

Selanio:

Since when?

Selan:

I dunno. Selan didn't notice at first cuz FFN doesn't allow that stuff when it's got real people in it and I don't pay enough attention anywhere else. But look! Someone made a site with all this stuff.

Selanio:

What's all this… this madness at the ends of the descriptions?

Selan:

That's just, you know, the pairings. All these things always have pairings. It's a little weird, but hey…

Selanio:

I-A-B-R? O-A-I-R? What the hell?

Xeno:

I'd assume that stands for 'Ira and Baron romance' and 'Omen and Ira romance'. Right?

Selan:

Yup.

Selanio:

Ughhh. What sorts of losers write this shit? … and what the hell does 'slash' mean?

Selan:

That means it's got you and Xeno making out! =D

Selanio:

Oh, *gods.*

Selan:

Or you guys and Apogee making out. Especially Xeno and Apogee. And I think I saw one involving Quantum.

Xeno:

Why, exactly, are you so excited about this?

Selan:

It's *hilarious!* My god, look at all these Sues! It's a comedy goldmine!

Selanio:

Gimme that. **(He takes the laptop and clicks the first fic he sees. He starts reading at some point in the middle.)** "As the Baron and Ira fled, escaping the scene of the crime, Omen hesitated, looking through the smokescreen at a coughing Apogee. He sighed. Part of him knew that he should just follow his comrades, but the rest of him just wanted to go back, take Apogee into his arms and—" Ahahaha, you're right, this is great! XD Look Xeno, you're so gay!

Selan:

Ugh, run-on sentences…

Xeno:

That's ridiculous! **(He steals the laptop and looks for something with Selanio in it. He starts reading.)** "Baron von Boom put on a tough exterior. But when it came down to it, he was just a tortured soul, longing for someone to love him." **(Xeno laughs and dodges Selanio trying to steal the laptop)** Ahahaha! Aww, Selanio, are you just a tortured soul?

Selanio:

Are *you* just after buttsex?

Xeno:

Jeez…

Selan (taking back her laptop):

Ooh, what's this one? Let's see… "Ira was looking forward to a shower after a long day's villainy. She took off her clothes, and opened the shower curtain, but saw that the Baron was—" Ehhh?! What the hell?!

Selanio:

Hn? Shto? **(He reads over her shoulder.)** It's a *porn!*

Selan (blushing furiously):

I didn't realize this site allowed that!!

Selanio (still reading it):

Ugh, why would anyone think I'd want to do *that* with *you?*

Xeno:

I notice you haven't stopped reading.

Selan (covering the screen):

Don't read that!! =O

Selanio:

Eh, it was lame anyway. u_u

Selan:

Another fic, another fic!! **(She finds something else.)** Ahh… a good old Sue. Good, safe sue.

Xeno (reading):

"Hoshi Sora Twila Hikaru was a high school student with superpowers. One day—" misspelled 'day', "—one day she found out the secret identities—" misspelled 'identities', "—of Ira's group and said—" misspelled 'said', "—and said 'I want to join your group, desu!'"

Selan:

Desu.

Selanio:

The porn was better.

Selan:

Of course you'd say that. -_-

Selanio:

Selanio means in terms of writing! The porn didn't have nearly as many typos.

Selan:

Like you were even paying attention. u_u

(She looks for something else.)

Xeno:

Seriously, why are we still reading these?

Selanio (pointing to the TV):

Look, now the airplane exploded!

Xeno:

Sweeeet.

Selan:
Were there annoying little kids on it?

Selanio:
Nah. Too bad.

Selan:
Pity. **(She looks at more fanfics.)** Maan, I wanna write one.

Selanio:
A fanfic?

Selan:
Yeah!

Xeno:
Is it possible to write fanfiction about yourself?

Selan:
I'm my own biggest fan!

Selanio:
Not like there's anyone else vying for that position.

Xeno:
Selan, don't you have a research paper to write?

Selan:
Homework later, fanfiction now!

(Xeno sighs. Selan holds her hands over her keyboard, ready to type… then sighs.)

Selan:
I don't know what to write.

Selanio:
Hah.

Xeno:
Now do your homework. u_u

-End: Episode fifty-three.

Lady Ira (while fighting Apogee):
Hey! Apogee! Did you know people are writing fanfiction about you?

Apogee:

Oh, God, no. o_O

054. Who's badass now?

(The scene is a small cubicle in an office somewhere in Washington DC. Clovis is sitting back in his chair, his feet on his desk, trying to balance a pen on his nose. One of his co-workers pokes his head into the cubicle.)

Osias:
Hey, Harlan. Have you seen Dave? He totally stole my stapler.

Clovis:
Who what now?

Osias:
Is that a no?

Clovis:
I'd say so.

Osias (standing there for a minute, watching Clovis balancing the pen):
You know, I'm pretty sure using your powers is cheating.

Clovis (has the pen floating above his nose by now):
Is not.

Osias:
So can I use your stapler?

Clovis:
So you can steal it? Hell no.

Osias:
You hardly ever do paperwork anyway, you don't need it.

Clovis:
I'm sure I'll need it. On the field.

Osias:
Yeah, you'll defeat evil by stapling documents at them.

Clovis:
Damn right.

Osias:
Well, you- **(He looks off to the side.)** Hey! Dave! You damn staple-thief!

(Osias runs off.)

Clovis: … (He sighs, picks up his stapler, and tries balancing that on his nose.)

(A couple minutes later, Clovis sees Osias walking past, stapler in hand.)

Clovis:
Hey. Adamina.

Osias (coming back):
Yeah?

Clovis:
… a *red* stapler?

Osias:
I… I ordered it special.

Clovis:
You watch too many movies.

Osias:
I know…

Clovis:
So is there, you know, anything going on?

Osias:
Nothing I've heard of. Slow week.

Clovis:
Ugh…

Osias:
Why are you even working here anyway? You've got superpowers, why don't you just take up superhero-ing? I'm sure the bosses could find you a good town to patrol.

Clovis:
Do I *look* like the superhero type?

Osias:
… you look like an emohero. Superemo. Something like that.

Clovis:
Fuck you.

Osias:
I'm just kidding. Anyway, the boss just told me to go get lunch for everyone. You wanna come with?

Clovis:
Why would I want to do that?

Osias:
So you can get outside and actually see the sun for once?

Clovis:
Good point. **(He gets up and walks over.)** Even though I know you just want me to tag along to help you carry shit.

(They start to leave.)

Clovis (pointing to the stapler):

Aren't you gonna put that back on your desk?

Osias:

That bastard Dave is just going to steal it again the minute I take my eyes off it.

Clovis:

All right then…

(They walk out to Osias's car and drive to the nearest fast food place. As they're in the middle of ordering their food, there's an explosion outside. The two look at each other and sigh.)

Clovis:

Ohm can take care of it. Let's just go.

Osias:

Can't. He's taking care of some hostage situation right now.

Clovis:

Fucking hell…

Osias:

Come on.

Clovis:

-_-; I'd better get a bonus.

(They walk out to find Reza standing atop a building, blowing shit up and preaching something about how any superpowered people should join him in destroying the inferior people, et cetera. Osias pulls out a gun.)

Clovis:

Dude, they gave you one of those?

Osias:

I do more than paperwork.

Clovis:

They hired me specifically *for* this shit and I don't have a gun.

Osias:

You can fuck with the laws of physics!

Clovis:
I'd rather just *shoot* people.

(Osias shrugs, and they approach Reza. Osias holds up his badge for Reza to see.)

Osias:
Reza! You are under arrest! Surrender now or we'll be forced to attack!

Clovis:
Even though we know you're just going to start blasting us.

Reza:
It's awfully refreshing to see someone with some common sense.

Clovis:
Thank you. I don't suppose you'll surrender, though?

Reza:
Of course not.

(Reza starts blasting at the two of them. Osias and Clovis dodge in two different directions, both avoiding getting hit. Osias opens fire, and Reza dodges the bullets, jumping off of the building and landing gracefully on the sidewalk below. Clovis, of course, holds out a hand and increases gravity, pinning Reza there.)

Clovis:
Hah. u_u Player one wins.

Osias:
Sweet. Er… have you got any handcuffs?

Clovis:
What, you don't?

Osias:
Dammit… Where the hell are the police when you need them?

Reza (getting back onto his feet, with great difficulty):
So you… you're helping these *normal* people?

Clovis:
They write my paychecks, so yes.

Reza:
Traitor.

(Reza manages to shoot a blast at Clovis. It hits him, and though it's a weak blast, it breaks his concentration and returns gravity to normal. Reza rushes forward and Clovis, who can't focus his powers on a moving target, jumps out of the way to avoid the villain's wrath. Reza shoots a blast at Clovis, who jumps again—a super-jump—to avoid. When he lands, Reza grabs him with an energy-hand and throws him. Clovis skids across the sidewalk, stopping somewhere near Osias. He gets to his feet, wiping some blood off his face.)

Clovis:
He's good.

Osias:
He's the organization's most wanted, so I'd assume so.

Clovis:
Give me your gun.

Osias:
But—

Clovis:
Just hand it over.

Osias (handing it over):
Okay…

(Reza, by now, has charged energy into his hands. He rushes at Clovis again and, seeing Clovis aiming the gun, zigzags a bit to make himself harder to hit. Despite this, Clovis lands a shot on Reza's right shoulder. Upon impact, the energy in his hand disperses. He stops, grabbing his shoulder and glaring at Clovis.)

Clovis (still pointing the gun, grinning):
Hah. Who's badass now?

Osias:
We'll only warn you once more, Reza! Surrender now!

Reza:

Kch. You can't rely on such dumb luck for long, I should warn you. **(Dark energy starts encircling him.)** We'll meet again. **(He disappears in a swirl of energy.)**

Osias:

W-wait, come back!

Clovis:

Give it up. **(He hands the gun back.)** Come on, let's get back to that food.

Osias:

Okay. **(They walk back to the restaurant.)** You were really amazing, by the way.

Clovis:

Hn.

Osias:

I wish I had superpowers like you.

Clovis:

You do, do you?

Osias:

Yeah. Imagine the good I could do.

Clovis:

Let's switch places, then.

Osias:

C-can we?

Clovis:

I wish. What did everyone want to eat, now?

Osias:

Ah… right. I'll order.

-End: Episode fifty-four.

Osias:

Kind of a crazy coincidence, him attacking right when we were there to stop him.

Clovis:

I'm more inclined to think we were set up. -_-;

055. Just okay?

(The scene is the campus. Selan is hanging out with Selanio in between class; both of them are sitting on the green. Suddenly, Tavvy runs up, stops, and sits down with them.)

Selan:
Uh…

Tavvy (short of breath):
Hi… ugh… gimme a second…

Selanio:
The hell're you running from?

Tavvy:
Cath. He's trying to… **(he pants)** to stop me.

Selan:
Stop you doing what…?

Tavvy:
Asking you out again. ^^;

Selan:
Um… you're not…

Selanio:

-_O; Green-hair-man doesn't know when to quit, does he?

Tavvy:

No, hear me out.

Selan:

Okay…

Tavvy:

Look, I… I know you don't like me like that. I know. It's just I have a really hard time giving up on things. And—and I'm almost ready to give up, I swear, it's just… I thought maybe it might make things easier for me if I make one last attempt. Like… one more date, and if you still feel the same way you do now after it, then that's it, I'm done. Okay?

Selanio:

Just leave her alone. u_u She's not interested.

Tavvy:

B-but…

Selanio:

Should Selanio repeat himself?

Selan:

Don't be mean, Selanio. =<

(Cath, by now, has caught up with Tavvy. He grabs Tavvy by the ponytail and pulls.)

Cath:

Oh, good, I got here just in time to *not* keep you from making an ass of yourself.

Tavvy:

Hey! Let go!

Selan:

Man, everyone's really against this, huh?

Tavvy:

=<

Cath:
Come on, man, let's just go.

Tavvy:
But! But!

Selan:
It's okay guys. ^^; I'll go.

Tavvy:
Really?!

Selanio:
What?!

Cath:
You're kidding me. -_-;

Selan:
Well, I mean, if it'll help Tavvy move on…

Cath:
Nothing will help this guy. He's hopeless.

Tavvy:
Th-the carnival's in town, we could maybe go there?

Selan:
Selan is cool with that. There's funnel cake in it for me, yeah?

Tavvy:
Sure!

Cath:
Won't that kill you?

Selanio:
It will. -_O

Selan:
It will not. u_u Anyway, I gotta get to class. When we going out?

Tavvy:
Umm… is tomorrow night good?

Selan:

Yup. Gimme a call with details, arrite?

Tavvy:

Okay!

(Selan leaves. Both Cath and Selanio glare at Tavvy.)

Cath:

You know how this is going to end.

Tavvy:

I—I know.

Cath:

I don't see how you think this could possibly be a good idea.

Tavvy:

I need to do it. =< For—for closure, you know.

Selanio:

Doesn't look like any sort of closure Selanio is familiar with.

Cath:

Seriously.

Tavvy:

L-leave me alone. =<

(Scene change!! It's tomorrow night, and Selan and Tavvy are at the carnival. But we're not paying attention to them. We're watching… Selanio? Indeed, Selanio seems to be following the two on their date, unbeknownst to them. As he's ducking behind a booth, however, he bumps into none other than Cath! Gasp.)

Selanio:

The hell are you doing here? -_O

Cath:

Just making sure Tavvy doesn't do anything… well, I shouldn't say stupid, since this whole date is stupid. I'm making sure he doesn't do anything stupider.

Selanio:

Selanio is doing the same.

Cath:
The hell do you care? I know you don't care about Tavvy and you know Selan can take care of herself.

Selanio (shrugging):
Selanio is getting tired of green-hair-man. He's so mousy and annoying. u_u Selanio must ensure that Selan does not fall for his mousy trickery.

Cath:
Whatever. How long've you been tailing them?

Selanio:
Not long. Selanio's had to keep his distance.

Cath:
Pfft. Amateur.

(Cath pulls out a set of headphones and puts them on. He toys with something hooked to the headphones.)

Selanio:
… you *bugged* them?

Cath:
Yup.

Selanio:
Sweet. You did something cool for once. What're they talking about?

Cath:
Let's see… Selan's asking what ride they should go on next and… oh, goddammit, Tavvy.

Selanio:
Shto, shto?

Cath:
He suggested the ferris wheel.

Selanio:
Aww, jeez. What a loser. She's not falling for it, is she?

Cath:
The line there is shorter than the other rides. She's going for it.

Selanio:
Damn. -_-;

Cath:
And now he's going to pour his heart out to her and she's going to rip it to shreds. -_-; Greeeat.

(Minutes later, Selan and Tavvy are in the Ferris wheel. Selan and Tavvy are sharing a cotton candy—mostly because Selan can't handle that much sugar on her own—while they ride the wheel. Eventually they find themselves waiting at the top of the wheel while people at the bottom are being let off.)

Tavvy:
So… have you been having fun?

Selan:
Yeah. n_n I love the carnival.

Tavvy:
So… um.

Selan (seeing what's coming):
Oh boy.

Tavvy:
Look, if you don't want to go on any more dates with me, that's fine. I just thought… you know, I'd try. One last time.

Selan:
Okay…

Tavvy:
I know Cath keeps saying that I'm hopeless and I can't move on, but I am. I'm over you, I am. It's just that I'm not good at giving up on things. I thought that, you know, if I asked you out one more time then I could say, like… it's in the hands of fate. Like, if you still don't like me then it wasn't meant to be, and if you change your mind then great. You know?

Selan:
Yeah. Sounds like a good enough idea to me.

Tavvy:
But I don't think anything's changed, has it.

Selan (looking away):
… I guess it wasn't meant to be.

Tavvy:
Okay.

Selan:
Just okay?

Tavvy:
Yeah.

Selan:
I bet you've got a bunch of girls just lining up to date you. n_n Hm?

Tavvy:
No… >_> Well…

Selan:
Well?

Tavvy:
Maybe one.

Selan:
One's all you need. n_n

Tavvy:
What about you? Is there anyone else interested in you?

Selan:
Eh, not that I know of.

Tavvy:
Really? **(He pauses, not sure if he should ask.)** What about Selanio?

Selan (nearly choking on her cotton candy):
Wh-what? Selanio?

Tavvy:
I was just wondering.

Selan:
What makes you think there's anything going on there?

Tavvy:

I-I don't know, I just thought…

Selan:

He's not interested in me. ^_^; I assure you.

Tavvy:

Okay…

(The ferris wheel moves, bringing them down to the ground. Meanwhile, where Cath and Selanio are spying on them…)

Cath:

…Well?

Selanio:

Well, what?

Cath:

Are you interested in Selan?

Selanio (crossing his arms):

Pfft. No. Selanio doesn't know what green-hair-man's going on about.

Cath:

… okay, all right. **(He takes off the headphones.)** Well, I guess that went as well as can be hoped. Tavvy doesn't seem devastated, Selan didn't do anything horrible, you're blushing like a schoolgirl—

Selanio:

I am not. >_<

Cath:

Anyway, I'm getting some carnival food and getting out of here. I'd recommend you get out of here too, before they see you and figure out you were stalking them.

Selanio:

Yeah, yeah.

Cath:

See you around.

(Cath walks off.)

(Selanio stands there for a moment. He sees Selan and Tavvy

passing by, and he ducks into the shadows to avoid being seen. As they walk off, disappearing into the crowd, Selanio grins.)

Selanio:

Take that, green-hair-man. u_u Your mousy charms get you nowhere.

(And with that, Selanio sneaks away, leaving the carnival.)

-End: Episode fifty-five.

056. *Um.*

(The scene is our villains' living room. They're watching the news. The anchor is talking about Ohm's latest exploits saving the president from a group of villains, when all of a sudden Selan jumps up.)

Selan:
H-holy craps! I know that guy!!

Xeno:
What? Who?

Selan (pointing):
Him! Look! Look what he's doing?

Selanio:
Ducking like a wuss?

Selan:
He's making a barrier!

Xeno:
What, like you?

Selan:

Yeah! I know this guy. He was in the experiment with me.

Xeno:

Are you sure? I mean, you had to have been like…

Selan:

We were four. I know. He looks different, what with the… being grown up. And all. But I know that stance. He has to duck and cover to make his barriers. It's like how I have to hold out my arms, you know?

Selanio:

Sounds pretty annoying. I'd prefer to have your power.

Selan:

^^; Well, if I remember right, he can hold his barriers longer…. Oh! You know what we should do, guys?!

Selanio:

Oh gods, here it comes…

Selan:

Shush, you. We should go pay him a visit! I bet his address is listed somewhere, hold on…

(Selan runs into her room. She's in there for a couple minutes, then comes out with a piece of printer paper.)

Selan:

I found him!

Xeno (taking the paper and looking at it):

Corbett Adamina, huh?

Selan:

We should go tomorrow and see him.

Xeno:

But he lives all the way in DC…

Selan:

It's only a couple hours away! And we've got a long weekend, so why not? Road trips are fun.

Selanio:

Eh, Selanio wouldn't mind doing something different

for a change.

Selan:
That's the spirit!

Xeno:
Okay, I guess it wouldn't hurt…

Selan:
Yaaaay!

(Time skip! It's the next day! The group have just finished their road trip, and they're standing outside the door to an apartment. Selan double-checks the paper.)

Selan:
This is it! Let's do this.

(She knocks on the door. There's a bit of noise on the other end of the door, and then a small voice inside says:)

Corbett:
Wh-who is it?

Selan:
You'll never guess! Open up!

Corbett:
O-okay…

(They hear the sound of way too many locks being unlocked, and then the door opens just a little bit. Corbett peeks out at them.)

Corbett:
Y-you're not here to r-rob me or anything?

Selanio:
Yes. Yes we are.

Corbett:
Eep!

(Corbett closes the door.)

Selan:
We're not! Selanio's just kidding! Corbett, it's me! Selan!

(There's a pause, and the door opens again.)

Corbett:
Selan?

Selan:
You know, from the experiment?

Corbett:
Prove it.

Selan:
Okay, okay. **(She holds out her arms and makes a barrier, then drops it.)** Eh? Eh?

Corbett:
Selan! …you look different.

Selan:
So do you. It's been what, 16 years?

Corbett:
Your hair is *red* now.

Selan:
I went through a couple colors. ^^;

Selanio:
Hey, hey, wait! This is my chance!

Xeno:
What?

Selanio:
I've been trying to figure out Selan's natural hair color for ages! She won't tell me.

Xeno:
You could've asked me, I'm psychic…

Selanio (looming over Corbett):
So out with it, what's her natural color?

Corbett:
Eep!

Selan:
Selanio, back off, you're scaring him. =< So you

haven't really changed, huh.

Corbett:
N-no… sorry…

Selan:
It's okay. Can we come in?

Corbett:
O-okay.

(Corbett allows everyone into his apartment, which is immaculately clean.)

Selanio:
So about Selan's hair color…

Corbett:
Sh-she's blonde…

Selanio:
Whaaat! **(He stares at Selan.)** … I can't imagine it.

Selan:
-_-; You know Cath's hair color? That's about it.

Selanio:
Sheesh.

Selan:
But anyway. Man! It's weird seeing someone I haven't seen since I was four. n_n

Corbett:
Y-yeah… weird…

Xeno:
So you guys ended up with the same superpower, huh?

Selan:
Well, similar. You guys know the difference already.

Corbett:
Other guys got… they got powers like, like fast healing, or invulnerability…

Selan:
Yeah, most of the powers people got from the treatment

were defensive things. **(She grins, looking sneaky.)** And as far as the government knows, me and Corbett are the only ones who didn't get powers.

Xeno:
I thought you'd said only a fraction of people got powers?

Selan:
That's the official story. **(She shrugs.)** Actually, if it wasn't for Corbett, they probably would've found out about my powers. I mean, if everyone in a study gets powers except one, you're gonna assume that one is just lying, right?

Xeno:
Yeah…

Selan:
But if two don't get it, then it's easier to just assume that there's a small chance that a subject just didn't get the thing. And since our parents were watching the whole time, they couldn't get too rigorous with their testing, so we got away scot-free.

Xeno:
Makes sense.

Corbett:
P-plus… plus, me and Selan, we… we didn't get along with the other kids… the adults, they assumed it was because we didn't have powers…

Selan:
It was actually because we were shy losers. ^_^ Right?

Corbett:
R-right… 6_6;…

Selan:
But man! If you're still as agoraphobic as you were then, I'm surprised you're a villain now.

Corbett:
Y-you know about that?!

Selan:
Why'd you think I came to visit? I saw you on the

news.

Corbett:

Y-y-y-you're not—you're not gonna turn me in?!

Selan:

Of course not! Just between you and me- **(she leans over and whispers, even though she doesn't have to)** I'm Lady Ira.

Corbett:

Wh-what!? No! You can't possibly be—

Selan:

Sure am. And this here's the Baron, and here's Omen.

Corbett (terrified):

Ah—ah—ah…

Selanio:

I think you broke him.

Corbett:

You-you guys are—are—

Selan:

Amazing, I know. u_u

Corbett (dropping on his knees):

You guys've got to help me!!

Selan:

Wha?

Corbett:

You—you guys are legends… if you could just talk to my teammates…

Selan (kneeling down to talk to him):

Talk to them about what? What's wrong?

Corbett:

I don't… I don't want to be evil, I don't…

Selan:

Are they forcing you to do it?

Corbett:

N-no…

Selanio (rolling his eyes):
Selanio doesn't see the problem, then.

Corbett:
It—it's just, it's just… they asked me to do it, they asked me… and I couldn't…I couldn't say no.

Selan:
Why?

Corbett (looking embarrassed):
Th-they're girls.

Selan:
You can't say no to girls?

Corbett (shaking his head):
But I don't want to do this… I'm terrified to get caught… **(His voice becomes very small.)** My brother works for the—that agency, the one that manages heroes. What would he think if he found out?

Xeno:
… okay, should we really be interfering if his brother works for those people?

Selan:
Of course we should! He needs our help. =<

Corbett:
They'll listen to you. They really admire you guys. Could—could you talk to them?

Selan:
Sure thing.

(Just then, Corbett's phone goes off. He opens it and reads a text message.)

Corbett:
Here, they want me to come meet them… could you come with me? I-In costume, maybe?

Selan:
Okay. Selanio, Xeno—

Corbett:
N-no! I-I mean… **(He whispers.)** They make me nervous.

Selan:
Okay… Uhh, you guys, just wait here. Don't touch anything.

(Not long after, Corbett is walking into a warehouse where Papaya and Dolly are waiting for him. Ira's behind him, but she's behind the door and out of view.)

Papaya:
Corbett! Man what took you so long?

Corbett:
W-well, I…

Papaya:
Come over here quick, we gotta plan our evil for the week and quick. =X I need to get home in time to surprise Silas with dinner.

Corbett:
Um, hold on, I…

Lady Ira (walking in):
Yo yo yo mah homies~

(Papaya and Dolly's jaws drop.)

Corbett (motioning at the girls):
Um… Ira, this is Dolly, and this is Papaya. Papaya is the leader.

Papaya:
Corbett, this is…

Lady Ira:
Yup, I know, you're all amazed to see me. u_u

Dolly:
Wow! You's the famous person! **(She rushes over, grabs Ira's hands and starts bouncing.)** You came to see us? Are you Corby's friend? Huh?

Lady Ira:
Yup. He and I go way back.

Papaya:
This isn't one of those things, like in sitcoms, where he just paid you to say you go way back?

Lady Ira:
Nah, this is for real. Except he didn't know I was Lady Ira cuz of the whole, you know, secret identity thing.

Papaya:
Wow. Corbett, you're officially awesome. u_u

Corbett:
Um… thanks?

Dolly:
It makeses sense, cuz they gots the same power, see?

Papaya:
Yeah. You guys related?

Lady Ira:
Nah. Just old friends. Anyway, Corbett brought me over here for a reason.

Dolly:
You gonna has a tea party with us?

Lady Ira:
I totally would if the guys weren't waiting for me. If I leave the Baron alone too long he'll start messing up Corbett's place for sure. ^^;;

Corbett:
… **(He whimpers.)**

Lady Ira:
Anyway, girls? Corbett wants to quit the villainy thing.

Dolly:
Whaaaat! **(She makes a sad face at Corbett.)** Don't you likeses us no mores? =<

Corbett:
W-well—I mean—er—

Papaya:
What's the deal, man? You're our defense guy! We need you!

Corbett:
But—but I—I mean—I don't—

Lady Ira:
He gets flustered. =< Anyway, he just doesn't want to do all this crime stuff. Some people aren't cut out for it, you know. And it's probably best to just let him go, since it's dangerous stuff if he breaks down or something.

Papaya:
I guess you're right…

Corbett:
So—so I—I can go?

Papaya:
Yeah, yeah… we'll find someone else.

Dolly:
We oughtta get 'nother girl! We cans be like… the no-boys-allowed club!

Papaya:
Hey, yeah… I don't think there are any other groups around who are all girls.

Lady Ira:
Nope, there's not. You'd really stand out if you had a trio of girls.

Papaya:
Sweet! Okay, that's what we'll do! u_u Hey, I don't suppose you'd be willing to ditch those guys you're with now and join us, eh?

Lady Ira:
Nah, no thanks. ^^; The Baron and Omen need me. They'd probably kill each other if I wasn't around.

Papaya:
Aw man. Well, it was worth a try. Okay! You two, you're not part of the group, so leave! We have top secret all-girl planning to do! Out, out!

Lady Ira:
Okay, okay, we're going. ^^; C'mon Corbett, let's go get some lunch =d

-End: Episode fifty-six.

057. Yo, boss.

(The scene is Lords Enterprises' headquarters. Cath is walking down the hall, carrying some papers. As he walks, Annick Zitomira comes out of a room and starts walking with him.)

Annick:
Hello there.

Cath:
Hm. Are you authorized to be here?

Annick:
Of course. **(He shows Cath his ID.)** I wouldn't be here if I weren't. n_n

Cath (looking over the ID):
Ah, the lawyer.

Annick:
You say that with such disdain.

Cath:
Can't say I like lawyers.

Annick:
Why's that?

Cath:
Don't trust 'em. They're about number two on my list of groups of people I distrust.

Annick:
Who has the honor of being number one?

Cath:
Politicians. Obviously.

Annick:
I see. What is it that you're doing, right now?

Cath:
Bringing the latest security reports to Kamaria.

Annick:
You mean Mrs. Lords…?

Cath:
… right. She still doesn't give off the 'wife' vibe, I can't break the habit of calling her by her old name.

Annick:
Of course. I don't suppose I could have a look at those reports?

Cath:
Absolutely not. They have nothing to do with lawyering and I don't have authorization to show them to anyone but my superiors. You're not my superior.

Annick:
Are they so secret?

Cath:
Not really. Just a bunch of all-clears and maintenance reports on our alarm systems. It's a matter of procedure; I'm not allowed to show them to anyone so I don't. u_u Besides…

Annick:
Yes…?

Cath:
In general, I hate people who ask unnecessary questions. So I gotta say, I'm not liking you very much right now.

Annick:
I see.

(They near the end of the hall. Dorcia walks out from a room and sees the two.)

Cath:
Yo, boss.

Dorcia:
You have the reports?

Cath:
What do you think these are, cookie recipes?

(He hands the papers over.)

Dorcia (looking over the papers):
Hm. As expected. **(She looks up at Annick.)** Was there something you wanted, Mister Zitomira…?

Annick:
Not really. I was just trying to get to know Mister Fordon here a little better. It's so good to be close with your co-workers, am I right?

Dorcia:
Hmm. If I recall, you are not scheduled to work today.

Annick:
I came by because I forgot my briefcase here yesterday.

Dorcia:
I see that you have it now, however.

Annick:
Yes. It's fine and in one piece, I'm glad to say.

Dorcia:
That is good to hear. Now, if your business here is concluded, I must ask you to leave. Those of us who are working today would prefer not to be interrupted by those

who are not.

Annick:
I understand. Sorry for the inconvenience. It was nice meeting you, Mister Fordon.

(Annick turns and leaves. Cath and Dorcia both try to pretend they aren't paying so much attention to him. Once he's finally gone, they relax.)

Cath:
I don't like him.

Dorcia:
Nor do I.

Cath:
Dalix hired him, didn't he?

Dorcia:
He did. He was hired a few days before we took Dalix down.

Cath:
Why the hell haven't we fired him, then? He could very well be a spy for Dalix, watching us and—

Dorcia:
I know. Damon has decided, however, to keep him around.

Cath:
Why? What could that idiot possibly be thinking?

Dorcia:
Well, firstoff, Mister Zitomira is an excellent lawyer. He has done some good things for the company. And second… I think that Damon is trying to observe Mister Zitomira.

Cath:
I see.

(There's a pause.)

Cath:
You know I could dig up any dirt on this guy you want. Just say the word and I'll do it.

Dorcia:

…

Cath:

If he's hiding anything, I can find it. You know I can.

Dorcia:

… no.

Cath:

Why the hell not?

Dorcia:

… it is dangerous. I can feel it. We would do well not to cross that man, for now.

Cath (frowning):

…

Dorcia:

It is best that we simply wait. There will come a moment when we can strike, and we shall do so with all our power. Until then, please try not to do anything stupid.

Cath:

And I suppose that's an order?

Dorcia:

Indeed. Now, go fetch me a coffee.

Cath:

I'm not your errand boy.

Dorcia:

Actually, Mister Fordon, you are. Now go. And no sugar or cream, please, I prefer my coffee black.

Cath (groaning):

Ugh… Fine… **(He walks off, muttering to himself.)** Where's Harlan in all this, I ask you? I miss seeing *him* run the stupid errands…

-End: Episode fifty-seven.

058. Your mom.

(It's a nice day out, and our villains are sitting atop a random building, having just blown up several nearby buildings. As they look over their remaining bombs, Apogee arrives. He hovers to meet them eye-to-eye.)

Apogee:
Not robbing any banks today?

Lady Ira:
Our heists have been really successful lately. We're running out of places to store the loot.

Baron von Boom:
But we felt like causing trouble, so we decided to go blow stuff up. u_u

Lady Ira:
Can't start slacking just 'cause we're doing so well. Am I right?

Apogee:
Oh, of course. Wouldn't want you three getting fat. u_u

Lady Ira:
Was that a crack at my weight? =< Cuz I'll have you know I weigh 130 pounds.

Baron von Boom:
Hahah, fatass.

Omen:
Shut up, you two, she's a twig. -_-

Apogee:
I was just making a couch potato joke.

Omen:
Sure, whatever. Let's get this over with.

Lady Ira:
Yeah! Ass kickin' time! Baron, Omen, go!

(Omen rips a banner off a nearby building and wraps it around Apogee. While Apogee's trying to break free, the Baron pelts him with energy bolts. The Baron moves in for the kill, but before he can get a punch in, Apogee breaks out of the banner and dodges, punching the Baron in the ribs while he's not guarding. The Baron doesn't skip a beat, however, and he kicks Apogee in the stomach and then proceeds to get him in a headlock.)

Baron von Boom:
Ha! Got you!

Apogee:
Hey! Let go!

Baron von Boom:
Say uncle!

Apogee:
Hell no!

Baron von Boom:
Say 'my mother wears funny hats and clown noses'!

Apogee:
-_-; What.

(Apogee breaks out of the hold and pushes the Baron away, throwing him into a nearby wall. Omen throws a car at him,

but he catches it and throws it back. Ira blocks the car, causing it to crash down onto the roof she's standing on.)

Apogee:
I'm glad that's not my car.

Lady Ira:
It looks new enough it should be covered by warranty.

Apogee:
You just threw it at me and left it on a roof! I think you voided the warranty!

Baron von Boom (swatting the car back onto the street—it lands with a shattering crash):
There, it's on the street. Warranty un-voided.

Apogee:
I'm pretty sure it doesn't work that way!

Omen:
Will you guys shut up and get back to fighting?!

(Everyone shuts up and looks at Omen, shocked by this outburst. He realizes how out of character this is for him, and looks away, embarrassed.)

Omen:
It's just… I've been stressed and these two haven't let me do my daily meditation, so I'm just really on edge is all…

Lady Ira: Poor Omen. =<

Baron von Boom:
Gasp! Omen actually has some fire in his eyes! Baron von Boom is curious. **(He starts poking Omen's forehead.)** Bother, bother, bother.

Apogee:
The hell're you doing?

Omen:
He's being annoying is what he's doing. >_<

Baron von Boom:
EXACTLY. Who knows, maybe you'll fight better if you're annoyed.

Omen:

And maybe *you'll* fight better if you stop poking me in the forehead!!

(As Omen says this, a transformer on a power line explodes.)

Lady Ira:

Ow, my ears…

Apogee:

Jeeeez. Okay, I'm gonna have to stop you now, Omen being annoyed is dangerous. -_-

(Apogee rushes toward the two of them. Baron von Boom picks Omen up and dodges.)

Baron von Boom:

No! Baron von Boom is near a BREAKTHROUGH. He could be some sort of superweapon and we might not even know it!

Omen:

Don't push me, Baron, you don't know what you're toying with!

Lady Ira:

Yeah! We already know he makes books fly like crazy if he's scared so I don't wanna know what he does when he's mad!

Apogee (shooting laser-eye-beams):

I'm pretty sure you're just gonna cause trouble for all of us.

Baron von Boom (jumping out of the way):

You're all WUSSES. Omen! Your mom's a whore!

Omen:

You think 'your mom' insults are going to do anything?

Baron von Boom:

They piss *me* off…

Lady Ira:

Really? Hey Baron! Your mom wore SHOES.

Baron von Boom:

-_- Lamest 'your mom' ever.

Lady Ira:
Your mom is the lamest 'your mom' ever.

Apogee:
-_- Why can't I have normal villains? Just a simple fistfight, that's all I ask.

Omen (closing his eyes):
I am calm. All the anger is leaving my body. Aummm…

Baron von Boom:
Shit! He's doing that hippie stuff! Gotta think fast. **(He pauses, then grins.)** Omen!

Omen (trying to concentrate):
I do not hear my less intelligent comrade's babbling…

Baron von Boom:
I ate all your leftover curry!

Omen:
You… you WHAT?

Baron von Boom:
It was gross. u_u

Omen:
My *mom* made that for me! Do you realize how much of a pain it is for her to mail cooked food to me all the way from where she lives?!

Lady Ira:
So 'your mom' insults *do* work…

Apogee:
Just gotta word them right, I guess…

Baron von Boom:
Eh, who cares. I was hungry. u_u

(Omen growls with rage. He opens his eyes, which are glowing with much greater intensity than usual…)

(Everything begins to shake.)

Lady Ira:
… I'm gonna go ahead and assume that I'm gonna have to hurt the Baron after this. -_-;;

(And… boom.)

-End: Episode fifty-eight.

(Our villains return home, battered and singed.)

Selan:
Stupid, stupid, stupid…

Selanio:
Selanio has a natural curiosity! I had to know what would happen, okay! I HAD TO.

Xeno (already in the kitchen):
Hey, my curry's still here!

Selan (glaring at Selanio):
Stupid, stupid, stupid…

059. Hey look!

(Tavvy's studying in the library when Danni walks up. She gives his ponytail a tug, then sits down across from him.)

Danni:
So when are you gonna ask me out?

Tavvy:
Eh?? What?

Danni:
Cath was saying how you wanted to ask me out.

Tavvy:
What? When did he say that?

Danni:
After he asked me out and I turned him down.

Tavvy:
Why'd you turn him down?

Danni:
Because he comes off as really sneaky.

Tavvy:
Ah.

Danni:
So, what, you *don't* want to go out with me?

Tavvy:
N-no—I mean—it's not that…

Danni:
Then what is it?

Tavvy:
I—I don't—er—

Danni:
You're shy. Is that it?

Tavvy:
Um.

Danni:
Okay, let's do it this way. Hey Tavvy, wanna go out with me sometime?

Tavvy:
…

Danni:
Hmm? Tavvy?

Tavvy:
… F-Friday?

Danni:
Friday's good.

Tavvy:
Ch-Chinese food?

Danni:
Sounds perfect. I'll leave you to your studying, okay?

Tavvy:
O-okay.

Danni:
See you Friday!

(She leaves.)

Tavvy (thinking):
What am I doing? I'm not ready to go dating anyone… but then again, she is really cute… and I'm pretty sure she's my type…

(Tavvy scratches his head, and smiles a bit.)

Tavvy:
Maybe Cath's right. I can't just wait around…

(Time skip!! It's Friday, and Tavvy and Danni are eating at a fancy Chinese restaurant. They seem to be having a merry old time.)

Danni:
… And I swear, Tavvy. Hygiene is like, optional for these people.

Tavvy:
It can't be that bad.

Danni:
You kidding? That class is like a biohazard. I've started coming to class wearing a surgical mask. They don't realize what the problem is. Even the teacher is smelly.

Tavvy:
You should start spraying Febreeze on them.

Danni:
I SHOULD. Totally.

Danni:
What about you? Got any awful classes to complain about?

Tavvy:
Not really. This semester's been pretty okay… I mean, my grades are awful, but it's not my teachers' faults. ^^;

Danni:
Hm? What's wrong with your grades?

Tavvy:
They're… pretty bad. 6_6 I've just been so busy, it's hard to keep up with things…

Danni:

Busy with what?

Tavvy:

Well, I've got this job.

Danni:

Doing what?

Tavvy:

I-I work for Professor Marika?

Danni:

Whoa. That intense guy? I had him Freshman year…

Tavvy:

Yeah, him.

Danni:

Ugh, you are a brave, brave little man. What all does he have you doing?

Tavvy:

Oh, this and that… I'm not supposed to talk about it. He's real secretive, you know.

Danni:

Aww, poor Tavvy… he's not buttfucking you, is he?

Tavvy:

Oh, ha ha.

Danni:

But really. If this job's ruining your grades and all, why don't you just quit?

Tavvy:

I hate it when people ask me that. ^^;

Danni:

Well?

Tavvy:

I'm not gonna quit, okay? I like my job, really.

Danni:

Oookay, if you wanna be a crazyman, I won't stop you.

Tavvy:
-_-;

Danni:
Well, anyway! So how's the art program treating you?

Tavvy:
It's got its ups and downs… **(He's about to continue, but his watch goes off.)** Ugh, not now…

Danni:
Hm? What?

(Tavvy glances at his watch, and then pretends to read a text message on his phone.)

Tavvy:
Shit. I'm sorry I'm sorry I'm sorry…

Danni:
Sorry about what? What's wrong?

Tavvy:
I have to go.

Danni:
But—our date…

Tavvy:
I—I'll take you on two dates next week! I promise! **(He rummages through his pockets, and hands her some money.)** This should cover dinner. Don't worry about the change. I'll call you later.

(He runs off. Danni sighs. She toys with her food as she waits for the bill to arrive, when…)

Random bystander near the window:
Hey look! Apogee's chasing some villain!

(Everyone rushes to the windows to watch. Danni goes also. Outside, Apogee and Quantum are in a flying chase. They stop right in front of the restaurant and exchange fire—Quantum shooting his lasers, and Apogee shooting his eye beams—before Quantum tries to escape and Apogee flies off in pursuit. The crowd stands watching them go, chattering amongst themselves. Danni stands watching, chewing her lip.)

Danni:

Hmm...

-End: Episode fifty-nine.

060. Nutjobs like you.

(It's a grey, humid day in Washington, DC. Ohm has just received word of Reza attacking some minor government buildings. He arrives on the scene to find the buildings in flames. Reza stands among the destruction, watching as the building burns.)

Ohm:

Reza!

Reza:

Oh, it's Ohm. Just you today, I see?

Ohm:

What the hell, man? Isn't this a bit too much destruction for such an unimportant target?

Reza:

Kch. As though you could possibly understand my goals.

Ohm:

Yeah, you're probably right. It's generally pretty tough for sane people like me to understand nutjobs like you.

Reza:
Hmph. **(He shoots a blast at Ohm, who blocks with his metal disc. He charges another blast, when all of a sudden the area around him goes dark, and he stumbles.)** What the…

Ohm:
Huh? **(He looks around and sees none other than Clovis Harlan perched atop a nearby building.)** Who the hell're you?

(Reza shoots a blast at Clovis, who dodges and jumps down from his perch. He lands next to Ohm, still trying to hold the gravity field over Reza.)

Clovis:
You can call me Agent Harlan. The agency sent me to give you a hand.

Ohm:
Oh, I see. You're one of those suits, huh?

Clovis:
Yup. But enough talking. See how he's radiating energy, there? He's trying to disrupt the field I'm holding him with. I'd recommend you attack before he gets loose.

Ohm:
Can do!

(Ohm hops onto his disc and flies a circle around Reza, shooting electric bolts at Reza as he goes around. Reza, however, shoots an energy-hand at Ohm and pulls him into the gravity field. Ohm ends up pinned to the ground.)

Reza:
Release the field or I'll finish this so-called hero.

Clovis:
Who's to say you won't kill him even if I do release the field?

Ohm:
Yeah, seriously.

(While Ohm can't move well, he's still able to manipulate a metal object on his belt, causing it to fly up and smack Reza in the head. This breaks the energy-arm Reza's holding Ohm down with, and Ohm uses his magnetism to adhere his feet to his disc, then flings his disc out of the field. It carries

him out as well.)

Clovis:
Good thinking, kid.

Ohm:
Yeah, well, you know what the physicists say. u_u Electromagnetism beats gravity every time.

Clovis:
Hm.

(Reza, by now, has recovered. He glares at Clovis.)

Reza:
By the way, Mister Harlan.

Clovis:
Hm? Did you say something?

Reza:
Don't think that I haven't done my research since our last little run-in.

Clovis:
Oh yeah?

Reza:
You're Clovis Harlan. You joined the Air Force when you were eighteen, and two years later disappeared… any fool would assume you'd been accepted into Black Ops—and I'm sure that's what you thought you were getting into…

(Clovis frowns.)

Reza:
But that wasn't the case, was it? It was something far less ordinary.

Ohm:
I wouldn't call Black Ops ordinary.

Clovis (ignoring Ohm):
You've made your point.

Reza:
Oh? Don't want me to continue? What are you going to do?

Clovis:
I said shut it.

Reza:
I suppose you'll kill me… just like you did to those scientists…?

Clovis (frowning more):
You'll scare mister static-cling over here.

(Reza grins—Clovis's concentration has faltered, and Reza's finally able to break the field around him. He leaps into the air and starts blasting at the heroes.)

Reza:
You were put into an experiment! For a year, they toyed with you, trying to figure out how to create super-powers, and after they gave you your powers, the experiments only got worse. **(He continues his assault, shrugging off the attacks Ohm is throwing at him and staying in constant motion so Clovis can't pin him down.)** They tried to figure out how your powers worked, and how they could replicate them in other subjects. It was brutal, wasn't it? Absolutely inhumane, what they did to you!

Clovis:
You think you're real clever, don't you?!

Reza:
And here you are, working for them! Working for the same government that commissioned the experiment that caused you so much pain! Don't you think there's something wrong with that?

Clovis:
It's none of your business!

Ohm:
I'm inclined to agree. **(He charges electricity into his hands.)** What this guy does is no business of yours!

(Ohm shoots a massive blast at Reza, who just barely manages to dodge. Reza responds with a blast of his own, which knocks Ohm into a nearby building.)

Reza:
I didn't find what I was looking for here, but I think I've made my point. I suppose I'll be on my way.

Ohm:
Wait-!

Reza:
Think about what I've said, Mister Harlan. I'm sure we'll be seeing each other again.

(Reza disappears in a swirl of black energy. Ohm punches the ground.)

Ohm:
Damn! Got away…

Clovis:
Shame. Well, I'm out.

Ohm:
Wait, you!

Clovis:
Hm?

Ohm:
Is what he said true?

Clovis:
Maybe.

Ohm:
If… if the government commissioned that experiment, then… why the hell are you working for the agency now?

Clovis (shrugging):
It's something to do, I guess.

Ohm:
Shouldn't you be holding a grudge or something?

Clovis:
Why? Everyone involved with the experiment is dead. There's no one left to be angry at.

Ohm:
…

Clovis:
See you.

(Clovis walks off, leaving Ohm to the business of trying to put out the fires.)

Clovis (under his breath):
Dammit Reza… you really know how to hit where it hurts…

-End: Episode sixty.

061. EXCLUSIVE

(It's a weekend, and our villains have just failed, once again, to take over the city. As they escape the scene, a stranger starts running up beside them, camcorder in hand.)

???:
Can I—Can I have a moment of your time?

Lady Ira:
What?

Omen:
Aren't you that chick from the news?

???:
Yep! Drei Valdis, channel seven news! Can I have a moment?

Baron von Boom:
No. We're kind of busy.

Omen:
Yeah, we're kind of trying to escape, here.

Lady Ira:
Wait, hold up hold up. **(She stops and looks around to make sure Apogee isn't anywhere nearby.)** What do you want?

Drei:
An interview.

Omen:
Why?

Drei:
Because it'd be just what our station needs! Think about it! Channel seven's EXCLUSIVE interview with the villains that continue to vex Apogee!

Omen:
Huh.

Lady Ira:
I do like vexing people…

Baron von Boom:
Look, lady. We are very dangerous people, understand?

Drei:
I know.

Baron von Boom:
I could snap you like a twig if I wanted to.

Drei:
I won't ask anything about your secret identities, I swear it.

Omen:
I don't know…

Lady Ira:
I think it's a good idea. We need better PR.

Baron von Boom:
We'd have better PR if you'd get off your fat ass and make that website.

Lady Ira:
But I'm so lazy.

(Drei starts setting up her tripod.)

Omen:

Plus we haven't been able to figure out how hosting will work. I mean, any host we sign up for is going to want a credit card number or a billing address…

Baron von Boom:

Can't we get a server and host it ourselves?

Lady Ira:

But then we'd need some mad 133t skillz to keep people from being able to trace its location. I'm sure the government's got some 1337 hax0rs to do that sort of thing.

Baron von Boom:

Can't Quantum fix us up? He knows computers.

Omen:

Yeah, like he'd really help us with something like that.

Lady Ira:

Well, maybe if we got Chandra on our side… hey! Are you recording?!

Drei:

No, no, ignore me, this is great! Footage of the dangerous villains having a normal, everyday conversation!

Baron von Boom:

Don't record that!

Lady Ira:

What is this, a nature documentary? "Here are the villains in their natural habitat…"

Drei:

C-can I?

Lady Ira:

Can you what?

Drei:

Film you in your natural habitat?

Baron von Boom:

Hell no.

Omen:
That's just not an option.

Lady Ira:
None of this Animal Planet stuff. Just interview us and let us go home.

Drei:
Oh, fine… Pff… hold on. **(She gets out some index cards and sifts through them.)** Ummm… So, okay. Let's talk to Ira first, since she's the leader. **(Pause.)** … you *are* the leader, right?

Lady Ira:
Duh.

Drei:
Okay. So, could you tell us a little bit about yourself?

Lady Ira:
Arrite. I'm Lady Ira, I'm amazing, and uh… I like kitties and video games. My superpower is that I can make barriers that can block anything. I'm also a badass ninja and have like smokebombs and kunai and stuff. Also my goggles are awesome.

Drei:
Can we hear anything about, like… your childhood, or your hometown, or your parents? Something a little more personal?

Lady Ira (smiling):
Absolutely not.

Drei:
Okay. **(She flips to another index card.)** So is the illustrious Lady Ira involved with anybody right now?

Lady Ira:
Hm? Like a boyfriend? **(She laughs.)** No, no. I've had offers, but no.

Baron von Boom:
Hah. What sort of loser would date this ugly hag anyway?

(The Baron pinches Ira's cheeks.)

Lady Ira:
Jerk! =<

Omen:
Behave, Baron. -_-;

Drei:
Moving on to the Baron! Hi Baron.

Baron von Boom:
Privyet.

Drei:
So you're from Russia, right? Or perhaps the Ukraine, or Belarus…

Baron von Boom:
Baron von Boom assures you that he is *not* Byelorussian.

Drei:
So what sort of stuff are you into?

Baron von Boom:
I enjoy explosions, destruction and mayhem. u_u

Drei:
Ah… right. So you were a solo villain before Ira and Omen came along, weren't you? What prompted you to join them?

Baron von Boom:
Omen's LIES.

Omen:
Oh, give it up already. -_-

Drei:
Ah… So Omen.

Omen:
No comment.

Drei:
But…

Omen:
No. Comment.

Drei:

Oh. =< Okay. So… **(She flips through her cards, skipping all her Omen-related questions.)** Serious question now. With the recent reappearance of Reza, there's been some talk that some villains might join forces with him. What are your thoughts on this?

Lady Ira (looking nervous):

Uh… well, he already approached us and we had to… decline.

Drei:

Oh?

Lady Ira:

Yeah. **(She pauses.)** Look, can you turn that off for a second?

Drei:

Huh? Oh, sure. **(She pushes something on the camera.)**

Lady Ira:

Is that actually off? Omen, check it.

Omen (looking at it):

Yeah, it's off.

Lady Ira:

Okay. Look, newslady. Don't ask us about Reza, okay?

Omen:

It's kind of a dangerous thing for us.

Lady Ira:

That guy is SCARY, alright? And there's a very real chance that if we say something that he doesn't like and you air it, he might just kill us in our sleep.

Drei:

Wow. So there're people even the villains are afraid of.

Lady Ira:

Well duh.

Omen:

Everyone fears *someone*.

Baron von Boom:
I don't. u_u

Lady Ira:
Liar, you lie. =<

Omen:
Seriously, man. We all know you're afraid of Indrid.

Baron von Boom:
He's *terrifying* and I don't know how you guys don't think so!!

Lady Ira:
I love how you admit that so freely. It's so unlike you.

Baron von Boom:
Indrid doesn't count anyway.

Drei:
Um…

Lady Ira:
Oh right, you're still here.

Drei:
I had a few other questions.

Lady Ira:
Nah, I think you're done here.

Drei:
But what about my exclusive? =<

Baron von Boom:
You want your exclusive? Here, turn the camera on.

(Drei turns the camera back on.)

Drei:
Okay.

(The Baron promptly flips the bird at the camera and then spouts off every word in the English language that isn't allowed on TV. He then starts to pull down his pants to flash the camera before Ira stops him.)

Lady Ira:
Okay, man, you've made your point! >_<

Drei:
O_o…

Omen:
Okay, now you've broken her little brain, and I'll be damned if *I* try and fix it.

Drei:
That… would make one hell of a sound byte… if censors didn't exist.

Baron von Boom:
Damn right.

Lady Ira:
Guys, let's get out of here while the Baron's pants are still on.

Omen:
Sounds like a plan to me.

Lady Ira:
Arrite, newslady, it's been… well, an experience. And now…

(She tosses down a smoke bomb and they escape.)

-End: Episode sixty-one.

Omen (coughing):
Was the smoke bomb necessary? Really?!

Lady Ira:
I HAD TO, Omen! It's a little thing called STYLE.

062. Swoon~

(Our villains are in the back of a car, driving down a snowy street. They're in Russia, approaching Selanio's old home. Selan is plastered to the window, watching the landscape go by, while Selanio is looking rather smug.)

Xeno:
Don't you think this is a little weird?

Selanio:
What is a little weird?

Xeno:
This! You've been gone from Russia for how many years, your parents have been dead for at least three years, and all of a sudden *now* you get word of some inheritance?

Selanio:
It takes time for word to get around, I guess.

Selan:
I dunno, it could be a bit suspicious…

Xeno (looking to make sure the divider between the back and front seats is up, still speaking in a low voice):
Look, Selanio… the villagers, they didn't really like your family, did they?

Selanio:
We kept the villain thing secret here, just like we do in America.

Selan:
But didn't you tell me you spent your last couple of years in Russia in some school in Moscow?

Selanio:
So?

Selan:
So you don't really know what the situation was before you went to America. I mean, why *did* you guys move to America?

Selanio:
Look, my father didn't blow his cover. He was too smart for that.

Xeno:
I'm just saying, maybe we should be careful while we're here.

Selanio:
You guys are being paranoid.

Selan:
Hey guys, what's that smell?

Xeno:
Hey, yeah, what is… **(He looks around.)** … uh, guys, have you noticed that there're no handles on the doors?

Selanio:
… I hate it when you guys are right.

(Selanio charges some energy into his hand, getting ready to blow the door off the car, but the three of them pass out before he can.)

(Xeno and Selan wake up on the side of the road some time later.)

Selan:
Ughhh. They friggin gassed us?

Xeno:
I guess so. Where are we?

Selan (looking around):
Uhh… looks like where we were, but, you know… no car. And no Selanio, what the hell?

Xeno (getting up):
Shit… I guess they *were* after him after all.

Selan:
We gotta help him! He might be- **(There's a rustling sound from within the forest.)** Eep! What was that?

Xeno:
Calm down. Probably just a squirrel or something.

Selan:
I heard about these Russian squirrels that ate a dog once… they've got a taste for blood, Xeno! Why do you think Selanio's so scared of them?

Xeno:
Oh, shush.

(A person comes out of the foliage. Selan jumps in front of Xeno and puts up a barrier.)

Selan:
Squirrel-vampire! AWAY FROM OUR BLOOD!

???:
Are you two Mister Roselani's friends?

Xeno:
Where did you bastards take him?

???:
I had nothing to do with it!

Selan:
Sure you didn't! **(She whacks the guy with her barrier.)** Now talk!

???:

Look, I'm here to help! I'm a friend of Selanio's father!

Xeno (to Selan):

You know, he doesn't have a Russian accent… I don't think he's one of the villagers.

Selan:

Maybe… and even if he is one of them, we don't have any other leads.

???:

I can hear you, you know.

Selan:

Silence! So who are you?

???:

I'm Daimhin. I used to manage the Roselani family assets.

Xeno:

What're you doing here, in the middle of nowhere?

Daimhin:

I heard about the villagers' plan. I was hoping to find you two.

Selan:

Okay…

Xeno:

So what's going on, then?

Daimhin:

The villagers finally found Mister Roselani. They've been wanting revenge for his family's villaining work for quite some time now. I think they plan to execute him.

Selan:

But they're a bunch of weasley little villagers and Selanio's a supervillain! They can't hurt him. They can't even restrain him!

Daimhin:

I wouldn't be so confident. They just received a shipment from the supervillain prison near Omsk.

Xeno:

So they may very well have restraints that can hold him.

Daimhin:

Yes. After all, they're very familiar with what his father can do. They wouldn't have called him here and risked a disaster if they weren't prepared.

Selan:

Okay, so this is a bad thing! Let's go save the Baron. =<

Daimhin:

Okay. This way. **(They start walking.)** There is one thing that's bothering me, though…

Selan:

Hm?

Daimhin:

Why'd they bring Selanio here? Why not his father, Mikhail?

Selan:

Well, see, his dad… both of his parents, they…

(She looks away.)

Xeno:

They died.

Daimhin:

What? When?

Selan:

A couple of years ago. It happened about a month before I met him.

Daimhin (sighing):

How has Selanio taken it? Has he been okay?

Selan:

Yeah. He's, you know… he's Selanio! I can't imagine him depressed, ever.

Daimhin:

You'd be surprised.

Selan:

…?

(Time skip! They've reached the outskirts of the village. It's a medium-sized village, far removed from other towns. Selan wonders if they get internet all the way out here. There's a huge mob formed around the town square—torches, pitchforks and all—where they have Selanio chained to a wooden podium. He's bound by his hands and feet, and he's struggling desperately to get free while screaming at the villagers in Russian. The leader of the mob is yelling over Selanio's voice, saying something to the rest of the mob.)

Xeno:

Selan, can you understand any of what he's saying?

Selan:

All Selan can pick out are words like "he" and "you". I only got a C in Russian class, remember!

Daimhin:

He's regaling the villagers with tales of what Selanio's father did and what they're going to do to Selanio for it.

Selan:

Ah.

Xeno:

So I guess we should bust in and lay down the hurt?

Selan:

Yeah, we… hey, no, wait! I have a better idea.

Xeno:

You do, do you?

Selan:

Hells yeah. Huddle up, guys, so I can whisper it to you all sneaky-like.

(Fade out as they do just that. A few minutes later, Selan and Daimhin have snuck behind the podium upon which Selanio is being held—there are no villagers behind it, probably because they wanted to see the carnage from the front or something—and they squeeze through a gap on the bottom of it to get inside the podium. Inside are four posts to which Selanio's restraints are bolted. Daimhin gets to work un-

bolting said restraints, while Selan knocks on the wood above her. Selanio looks down, and sees Selan looking up at him from between the cracks in the wood. She motions off to the side. He looks up and sees Xeno off at the corner of the crowd. Xeno waves, and Selanio grins and begins to laugh maniacally. He starts yelling at the villagers in Russian.)

Daimhin (still unbolting the chains):
Sounds like he's got some idea of what we're up to.

Selan:
Oh good.

(Xeno looks around to make sure no one's looking his way, and then proceeds to use his powers to make anything that isn't bolted down start floating and flying around. Selanio laughs again and starts talking again.)

Daimhin (translating Selanio's words):
'You thought it would be so easy? You idiots have no idea how powerful I am,' Okay, his feet are free.

(He moves on to the next post.)

Selan (watching the mob from through the cracks):
Looks like they're falling for it. Eep, guns! Forgot about that possibility. Hold up.

(She puts out her arms and makes a barrier that envelops the entire podium, Selanio included. The villagers try to shoot at Selanio, but their bullets are unable to break through. The villagers are now thoroughly terrified. Selanio continues to taunt them in Russian.)

Daimhin (translating again):
'Compared to you tiny people, I'm like a god!' Boy, his ego's certainly inflated, hasn't it?

Selan:
Yeah, he's pretty much the exact opposite of modest.

Daimhin:
Okay, he's free.

Selan:
Sweet. **(She knocks on the wood again.)** You're free, man! Go kick some ass!

(Selanio grins down at her, then returns his attention to the mob and says something.)

Daimhin:
He said, 'It's time you all learned what happens when you anger a god.'

(Selanio leaps from the podium and into the crowd, his hands charging energy. The crowd disperses, terrified, and he proceeds to run about town, destroying everything in sight and laughing all the while. Selan, Daimhin and Xeno all meet up in front of the podium and watch the destruction.)

Xeno:
Well, that went well. After this I don't think they'd ever have the guts to try something like this again.

Selan:
Yup.

Xeno:
Not that we'd ever fall for it again if they did try anything.

Selan:
Yeah, well, this was more dramatic. Plus, we get to watch Selanio being crazy evil!

Daimhin:
He really is so much like his father. It's eerie.

Selan:
His evil laugh is amazing, I have to admit. Must be breeding. You don't perfect a laugh like that in just one generation.

Daimhin (laughing):
Selanio and his father used to practice their laughs together.

Selan:
That's adorable. **(She smiles, watching as Selanio merrily destroys the town. She leans against the podium.)** Hot damn, guys, don't tell Selanio I said this, but when he gets this evil I just wanna swoon.

Xeno:
…

Selan:
What's that face for?

Xeno:
Never talk like that again, please. -_-;

Selan:
What? I'm just saying Selanio's an awesome villain.

Xeno:
Whatever. -_-

(A few hours later, Selanio, Selan, Xeno and Daimhin are walking away from the village, in the direction of Selanio's old house.)

Selanio:
Man, Daimhin, I haven't seen you in ages!

Daimhin:
Tell me about it. Last time I saw you, you were still shorter than me. Now you're a giant.

Selan:
Short… Selanio… buu, I can't imagine it.

Selanio (glaring):
Because I just *congealed* somewhere?

Selan:
Ahaha, so Kesava told you about that?

Daimhin:
Oh, how is Kesava doing? Did he move to America too?

Selanio:
Da. He's in college right now, studying animals or something dangerous like that.

Daimhin:
I see. And what about you?

Selanio:
I'm going into grad school soon. Chemistry.

Daimhin:
That's my boy.

Xeno:
Not to interrupt, but do you have any idea how the villagers figured out where Selanio was living?

Selan:
Hey, yeah. That's pretty important.

Daimhin:
I'm not sure, myself… I mean, they already knew about the Roselani family's superpowers, but—

Selanio:
Wait, wait—what?

Daimhin:
You didn't know? That's why your family fled to America, because their identities got exposed.

Selanio:
But—but dad was too smart for that! He was always so careful—

Daimhin:
That's right, he was. That's why he sent you to Moscow—because he realized the villagers were trying to find his identity and he didn't want anything to happen to you if they did.

Selanio:
Holy hell…

(They arrive at the house and enter. Daimhin wanders into another room while Selanio looks around, looking somewhat melancholy.)

Selanio:
I guess it makes sense…

Selan:
What does?

Selanio:
When we left, I asked if we would ever come back and visit and he said no, we wouldn't. I guess what he meant was that we *couldn't* come back.

Selan:
Oh…

(Daimhin comes back into the room with an envelope.)

Daimhin:

Here. I don't know how the villagers found you, but this might be a hint. A man came around asking about the villains of the area and left this. He might've had something to do with it.

Selanio (taking the letter):

… damn, man, do you *live* here now?

Daimhin:

Only on vacations. I spend most of my time in Irkutsk these days.

Selan:

This guy who left this, did you know him?

Daimhin:

No. He came around asking questions about Selanio's family. I didn't tell him anything, but he came back after visiting the village and left this, saying that it was for someone named 'the Baron'. I haven't opened it. I surmise the villagers probably weren't as tight-lipped as I was.

Xeno (suspicious):

What did he look like…?

Daimhin:

He had dark hair, and a tattoo under his left eye.

(Selan, Selanio and Xeno all look at each other. Selanio rips the letter open.)

Daimhin:

… what? Do you all know him?

Selanio (reading the letter aloud):

'If you are reading this, then my fears have proven to be well-founded. I came to this town to do some research on the villains that once lived here, but when talking to the villagers I think my interpreter might have let something slip about the Baron. Something about him having the same powers as the villain here, I'm not quite sure myself. My Russian is awful, as I've told you in the past.
I just want to say I'm sorry for putting you in any danger, it absolutely was not my intention.
Signed, Reza."

(Selanio crumples up the letter.)

Selanio:
'Not my intention', my ass!

Selan:
Shit. Guys, do you think Reza knows Selanio's identity now?

Xeno:
Probably.

Daimhin:
But it said—

Selanio:
This letter is full of lies.

Selan:
It wouldn't be much of a stretch for him to figure out his identity. I mean, he comes here and hears about some villain with the same powers as Selanio who fled to America, who had a son… and then all he has to do is say, "Oh hey guys, I know that guy's kid. Here's where he lives!"

Xeno:
Why would he do that, though? I mean, he hates normal people, no way he'd risk letting a superpowered person get killed by stupid villagers.

Selan:
No, man, I get it. He's trying to freak us out. Like, he probably figured we'd come along too and bail the Baron out. He's just trying to get us to hate normal people, or to get us paranoid about what would happen if we got caught back home.

Selanio:
Dirty, underhanded sonofabitch…

Selan:
It's totally not cool. If he thinks tricks like this are gonna get us to join him, then… well, I guess it's no wonder why he doesn't have that army he wants!

Xeno:
Seriously.

Daimhin:
I'm a little lost.

Selanio:
It doesn't matter. -_-; What's important is that the villagers got what was coming to them and we're not falling for this trick.

Selan:
I wish Reza could get what was coming to him. =<

Xeno:
We don't stand a chance against him, so I don't think that'll be happening. -_-

Selanio:
One of these days, we'll get him. This is a promise.

Selan:
Yeah! We will.

(Fade out, time skip to a couple of hours later. Selanio's sitting on the bed in his old room, absently holding a small plush toy. Selan opens the door, having come back from getting dinner in town. She's holding a box.)

Selan:
Hey, we're back. n_n Nice of you to leave one restaurant still standing.

Selanio:
Hm.

Selan (walking in):
We brought you some leftovers. Sorry you couldn't come along.

Selanio:
Selanio isn't very hungry.

Selan:
Oh, don't be like that. I know you haven't had real Russian food in years, there's no way you're not hungry for it.

Selanio:
I know it's not going to be as good as mom's cooking.

Selan:

Oh. **(She sets the food down on the nightstand and sits down next to Selanio.)** Are you okay?

Selanio:

… I can never come back here. I always thought that maybe someday I could return, but I guess once we leave then that's it.

Selan:

Selanio…

Selanio:

I really miss them, you know.

Selan:

Your parents?

Selanio (nodding):

You and Xeno don't know what it's like; both of you still have your parents. It… it's hard. We were very close.

Selan (hugging Selanio):

It's okay. I'm sure they're watching you from on a cloud somewhere.

Selanio:

Do you think… **(He pauses, chewing his lip.)** Do you think they would be proud of me?

Selan:

You kidding? I bet they were cheering you on the whole time you were rampaging today! You were amazing!

Selanio:

Eto pravda?

Selan (nodding):

Da! Pravda!

(Selanio smiles, then pushes Selan away.)

Selanio:

Now get off of me, I might catch your *loser-ness.*

Selan:

Hey!

Selanio:
And hand over that food. I'm starving after all.

Selan:
Hah, I knew it. You were just being emo. u_u

(Selan hands over the box and Selanio starts eating.)

Selan:
So we were thinking we could hop on a train tonight and make it to Moscow by tomorrow, maybe?

Selanio:
Huh? Why?

Selan:
Cuz I've always wanted to visit Moscow, that's why! And since me and Xeno bailed you out, we figure you owe us a tour of the city at least. Maybe you can treat us to a big fancy dinner too?

Selanio:
Hey! What if I refuse?

Selan:
Then I'll just have to sic the squirrel on you when we get home. >3

Selanio:
Grr… fine…

Selan:
Yay! Sweet.

-End: Episode sixty-two.

063. Shady people.

(It's a nice day in Washington, DC. Tynan and Cath are eating some takeout in a park.)

Tynan:
Nice of you to come visit.

Cath:
Well, I had some days off, so what the hell, right?

Tynan:
Days off from work or days off from school?

Cath:
Work. Fuck school.

Tynan (sighing):
Of course…

Cath:
So how've you been, man? Not getting your ass kicked, are you?

Tynan:
Nah, I've been all right. It's been pretty busy around here.

Cath:
Reza, I assume?

Tynan:
Yeah.

Cath:
I hear you've been getting help from the Agency.

Tynan:
Where'd you hear that?

Cath:
I know people.

Tynan:
The only people you know are shady people and Tavvy. Spill it.

Cath:
Hey, who's to say there aren't shady people in the agency?

Tynan:
I suppose. **(He thinks for a moment, chewing his food.)** You know a guy named Harlan?

Cath:
Ahh, you figured it out.

Tynan:
I knew it! He certainly seemed shady enough to be one of your friends.

Cath:
One, I wouldn't call him my *friend*. Two, what the hell, why do I have to only know shady people? I know not-shady people!

Tynan:
Name one who isn't Tavvy.

Cath:
Danni.

Tynan:

Okay, name *two.*

Cath:

… you?

Tynan:

I'm hella-shady and you know it.

Cath:

You are not, you're a lame goody-two-shoes. Anyway, how do you know Harlan?

Tynan:

He's the one who helped me out, man.

Cath:

Seriously? Agh, that jerk. He said they'd sent someone to help you, he didn't say that someone was *him.*

Tynan:

How'd you get to know someone in the Agency, anyway? Have you been in trouble with them or something?

Cath:

Jeez, why do you always assume the worst? He used to work with me at Lords, okay?

Tynan:

Seriously? Man, I wonder if the Agency knows that.

Cath:

Who knows. You gonna eat that egg roll?

Tynan:

Yes I am, back off. Do you know anything about that guy's past?

Cath:

Apparently he was in the Air Force or something, I dunno. I was never really interested enough to ask.

Tynan:

Hn…

Cath:

Why?

Tynan:
    No reason.

Cath:
    You know something I don't, don't you?

Tynan:
    No.

Cath:
    You know you can't get away with lying to me.

Tynan:
    Same to you, but you still try.

Cath:
    Come on, what do you know? Is it anything I can blackmail him with?

Tynan:
    I'm pretty sure that if you tried, you'd end up dead, so no.

Cath:
    Tell me, already! What is it?

Tynan:
    I shouldn't say. The only reason I know is because Reza said it, and Harlan didn't seem all to keen on me hearing it.

Cath:
    I don't care if he *wants* me to know.

Tynan:
    -_-; Grow up, Cath.

Cath:
    Ugh. You're so lame sometimes. -_- Fine, I'll just research it myself.

Tynan:
    Good luck. I tried and had no luck, and I have access to Agency files! I don't know how Reza figured it out.

Cath:
    Oh, like the Agency keeps anything secret in writing.

Tynan:
Point. Ugh… What I really want to know is if I can trust the guy.

Cath:
Who, Harlan?

Tynan:
Yeah. I mean, if he's the Agency's current enforcer, I'm probably going to be seeing more of him, and it's clear that Reza wants to get this guy on his side. Can I really trust him not to turn on me?

Cath:
As much as I hate to say this… yeah, you really can.

Tynan:
Why would you hate to say that?

Cath:
Because he's a dick and I hate him?

Tynan:
Okay…

Cath:
Anyway, this guy, he's got this really strict honor code. He won't admit to it, but he does. I don't think you ever have to worry about him joining Reza, he'd sooner jump off a cliff.

Tynan:
That's good to know.

Cath:
Just hope you don't have to fight any villain chicks with him, he's got this thing against hitting women. He'll get all emo on you.

Tynan:
You know this by experience…?

Cath:
He put Lady Ira in the hospital and then promptly quit the company. I mean, I tried to tell him like, hey, she's a villain, what's it matter? But would he listen to me? Nope.

Tynan:
Seriously?

Cath:
Yep. If he had actually been *trying*, he probably could've killed her.

Tynan:
Huh. **(He pauses.)** And where were you?

Cath:
Next to him, telling him to hurry the hell up.

Tynan (shaking his head):
Cath, you're a horrible person.

Cath:
What? Like I said, she's a villain. And annoying.

Tynan:
Horrible, horrible person.

Cath:
Jeez, whatever.

(Tynan's watch goes off.)

Tynan:
Holy hell, what is it now? **(He looks at it.)** Oh good, just a bank robbery. Wanna come?

Cath:
Why would I want to do that?

Tynan:
Because beating up robbers is fun? Come on, if you do it I'll tell you how to do the flying trick.

Cath:
You always say that but you never spend more than five minutes trying to show me.

Tynan:
Okay, I'll spend ten minutes this time! Come on, we gotta go!

Cath:
Okay, okay…

(The two run off, leaving their food behind—except for an egg roll, which Tynan wolfs down as they run to get in costume.)

-End: Episode sixty-three.

064. This stinks.

(The scene is the Professor's office. Tavvy and the Professor are in there, sitting at the desk. Tavvy looks nervous.)

Tavvy:

So these Agency guys… they're not real scary, are they?

Marika:

No scarier than me.

Tavvy:

But you're *terrifying.*

Marika:

Am I? Oh well. Anyway, go along with this. Remember, they sign your paychecks. You've gone this long without an inspection because you've technically been classified as my apprentice, but that period's expired. After this, you'll officially be an independent superhero.

Tavvy:

Will they pay me more?

Marika:

If they don't think you're entirely useless.

Tavvy:

Gee, thanks.

(There's a knock on the door.)

Marika:

It's open, come in.

(The door opens and Clovis and Osias walk in. Osias smiles at the two in the room, while Clovis looks like he doesn't really want to be there.)

Osias:

Good morning, gentlemen.

Tavvy:

Hey! You're…

Clovis:

Yeah, yeah, nice to see you again and all that.

Osias:

You've met?

Clovis:

Yeah. On that space mission. Apogee and the Professor were—

Osias:

You've met the Professor, too?! **(He whispers to Clovis.)** Do you realize how much I had to beg to get this assignment just so I could see him, and here you've already met him?!

Clovis:

Why do you think they sent me too? Probably 'cause I know them.

Osias:

Damn… Okay, okay. **(He turns to face them again, pauses, then faces Clovis again.)** What space mission?

Clovis:

… we're getting off topic. Hey, Professor.

Marika:
Yes?

Clovis:
Get the hell outta here.

Osias:
H-Harlan! Be more polite.

Clovis:
As a matter of procedure, we can't have anyone but us and the superhero in question in here. Sorry, Professor, but you gotta go. There, polite enough for you?

Osias:
Jeez.

Marika:
Yeah, yeah…

(Marika gets up and leaves.)

Clovis:
All that begging just to see him for a minute, huh?

Osias:
It's worth it! That guy was my hero when I was a kid!

Tavvy:
Me too. ^^; Now I'm more scared of him than anything.

Clovis:
Yeah, he seems pretty unpleasant. **(He turns on a tape recorder.)** Okay, kid, state your name, both superhero name and given name, for the record.

Tavvy:
Um… Apogee. Tavarius Imogene.

Clovis:
Right. Adamina, measure him.

Tavvy:
Eh? What?

Clovis:
We need to have certain physical information on record, like your height.

(Osias gets out a measuring tape and measures Tavvy.)

Osias:

Five feet, five inches.

Tavvy:

-_-; Does that really have to go on record?

Clovis:

What, you think that if we don't say it, no one'll notice? Embrace your shortness, kiddo. Now what's your natural hair color?

Tavvy:

Brown.

Clovis:

Any medical issues? Allergies, disorders?

Tavvy:

No.

Clovis:

Did your parents have any medical issues that you might inherit later?

Tavvy:

I don't think so…? Oh! But Indrid said my body might reject my superpowers again. But he'll take care of that.

Clovis:

Again?

Osias:

Indrid?

Tavvy:

It happened once before. It kinda hurt. ^^;

Clovis:

Right then. Have you had your blood pressure checked recently?

Tavvy:

It was normal, I think. Guys, I'm pretty sure my superpowers keep me pretty healthy.

Osias:

We know. We're just following procedure.

Clovis:

Let's move on. What about weaknesses? Got any of those?

Tavvy:

Not that I know of. I mean, what sort of things are people usually weak to?

Osias:

Radioactivity?

Clovis (rolling his eyes):

Everyone and their mom is weak to that. I don't know, some people get weak in the presence of like, rare metals or are weaker at night or something.

Tavvy:

Oh. Well, I don't.

Clovis:

Convenient enough. State your current known nemeses.

Tavvy:

Um… there's Ira's group, which is Lady Ira, Baron von Boom and Omen. Then there's Quantum and Chandra, and I think Reza counts too, doesn't he?

Clovis:

That he does. Arrests?

Tavvy (flinching):

Hundreds of non-superpowered criminals. Um… the Professor said that the invasion counts as an arrest too.

Clovis:

Okay, I'll have them mark that.

Osias:

Invasion? Why am I the only one out of the loop, here?

Clovis:

Don't know, might wanna ask the boss-man. Was there anything else we had to ask?

Osias:
No, all the rest of it's just the paperwork and all, and he already did that…

Clovis (turning off the recorder):
What a waste of time. Your tax dollars at work, guys!

Tavvy:
Is that it?

Osias:
You know, now that the recorder's off, can you guys let me in on all this space… invasion… Ingrid talk?

Tavvy:
Indrid.

Osias:
Whatever.

Clovis:
Look, there was this alien invasion thing a while back, Tavvy and some other guys had to take care of it, and the Agency sent me to keep an eye on the whole thing. And Indrid… doesn't exist.

Osias:
I never heard about any of this.

Tavvy:
Must've been real secret.

Clovis:
… you know, now that I think about it…

Tavvy:
Hm?

Clovis:
From what I gather, the only people who know of Indrid are Tavvy and Omen, and then the Professor, cuz he knows Tavvy, and Ira and the Baron, cuz they know Omen. And then me.

Osias:
And me?

Clovis:
Shut up. And Indrid's got the power to, like, wipe memories, he can see the future and knows everything.

Osias:
What're you getting at?

Clovis:
How the hell does our organization know Indrid? And how do we actually have active channels of communication with him?! Don't you think he'd avoid having to reveal his existence to the government? He certainly has the means to keep it secret, so what the hell is his reason for dealing with our agency?

Tavvy:
Um… wow. That's a good question.

Clovis:
This stinks something awful. C'mon, Adamina, I'm getting to the bottom of this.

(Clovis walks out.)

Osias:
W-wait! **(He hastily gathers the tape recorder and the papers.)** Thank you for your time, we'll be in contact. Dammit, Harlan, wait up!

(Osias leaves. Marika comes back.)

Marika:
Hmm. Looks like that was a little more interesting than usual. What'd you say to piss that one off?

Tavvy:
N-nothing.

Marika:
Nothing? Really.

Tavvy:
Really! I swear!

Marika:
Sure. Now then. **(He tosses Tavvy's watch at Tavvy—he's been holding onto it the whole time.)** This's been going off. Better take care of it.

Tavvy:

Aw, man.

(Tavvy runs off to save the city once again, passing a brooding Clovis and a confused Osias as he leaves.)

-End: Episode sixty-four.

065. I'm glad.

(It's a Wednesday night. Tavvy and Danni are waiting in line at the campus theatre.)

Tavvy:
Man, I'm so excited to see this movie.

Danni:
I can't believe you haven't seen it before!

Tavvy:
I know, I know… it's just, every time I try to see it, something comes up and- **(his watch beeps)** - oh hell. -_-

Danni:
What?

Tavvy (pretending to look at his phone):
… something just came up.

Danni:
What? But you've been looking forward to this all week!

Tavvy:
I know…

Danni:
Whatever it is, can't it wait?

Tavvy:
Well… **(There's the sound of an explosion outside.)** N-no, it can't! See you!

(He runs off.)

Danni:
-_-; Sigh…

(Scene change! It's the next day, and Danni and Tavvy are eating together in the cafeteria.)

Tavvy:
… but that's just how things go, I guess.

Danni:
What, you kidding? Man, if I'd gotten ripped off like that, I'd come back to the store with a lawyer.

Tavvy:
Well, I was in a hurry so I didn't have time to make a big deal out of it… **(He smiles.)** Plus, the next day Baron von Boom blew the place up.

Danni:
Apogee wasn't able to stop him?

Tavvy:
Guess not. **(He chuckles.)**

Danni:
Well, I guess that's what they get. It's karma. u_u

Tavvy:
I think so too. n_n

Danni:
So—

(Tavvy's watch goes off.)

Tavvy:

Um! I—I almost forgot! I have a meeting with my anatomy professor today!

Danni:

Right now?

Tavvy:

Y-yeah. Sorry.

(Tavvy runs off.)

(Scene change again! Danni, Tavvy and Cath are hanging out on the green.)

Danni:

And then he's all like, "*Really?*"

(Tavvy and Cath laugh.)

Tavvy:

That reminds me of this time I- **(His watch goes off.)** Agh! You can't be serious!

Danni:

You have to go again? -_-

Tavvy:

I'm so sorry.

Danni:

Go on, then.

(Tavvy leaves)

Cath (watching him go):

So he's been doing that a lot, eh?

Danni:

Does he always do that?

Cath:

Yup.

Danni:

You know…

Cath:

Hm?

Danni:

Something's bothering me.

Cath:

What's that?

Danni:

Well, have you ever noticed how, whenever Tavvy runs off, Apogee usually shows up somewhere?

Cath:

…

Danni:

It's weird. There hasn't been a single time where Apogee's somewhere that I've been able to get ahold of Tavvy.

Cath:

Huh.

Danni:

I mean, I might be crazy here but… do you think that maybe… Tavvy is Apogee?

Cath:

… Well, the only thing I can really tell you is, **(he stands up)** sometimes it's good to just not ask questions.

Danni:

…

Cath:

See you around.

(Cath walks off.)

Danni:

…

(She frowns and makes a face at Cath.)

(One more scene change, guys! Danni and Tavvy are playing video games at Tavvy's apartment when, surprise surprise, Tavvy's watch goes off. He leaves.)

(Hours later, Tavvy is stumbling back to his apartment, battered and exhausted after fighting off first Ira's group, and then Quantum. He walks into his apartment and is surprised to see Danni still there.)

Danni:
Sup.

Tavvy:
Huh? Danni?

Danni:
Damn, look at you. Get hit by a bus or something?

Tavvy:
You're still here?

Danni:
Well, I had my laptop with me, so I figured I might as well stick around and do my homework…

Tavvy:
…

Danni:
Are you okay?

(Tavvy walks over and hugs Danni.)

Tavvy:
I'm so used to coming here, exhausted and miserable, and having no one here to greet me. I'm… I'm glad you're here.

Danni (returning the hug):
… now are you going to stop running out on me?

Tavvy:
Er…

Danni:
Kidding. n_n

Tavvy:
n_n;; Aha… haha… -_-;

-End: Episode sixty-five.

066. I wonder.

(Selanio and Selan are hanging out on the green. Selan's working on her Japanese homework while Selanio's just lying there, relaxing.)

Selan (writing):
Haya… ku… o… ki… su… gi… ma… shi… ta.

Selanio (yawning):
Znachit tak…

Selan (still writing):
Ni… hon… go… de… hana… shi… ma… shi… chiisai yo… u.

Selanio:
Skolko seichas vremeni?

Selan (looking at Selanio):
Ima niji han desu yo.

Selanio:
Ah, spacibo.

(Stesha has walked up to them, but they haven't noticed.)

Stesha (sitting down):
Do either of you understand each other at all?

Selan:
I think he asked what time was it…

Selanio:
Selanio is pretty sure she said it was two.

Selan:
Two thirty.

Selanio:
Close enough. The hell do you want, Zitomira?

Stesha:
I just thought you two sounded dumb is all.

Selan:
We're *multicultural*, jerk!

Stesha:
Whatever. Anyway, I thought I'd apologize for the whole, you know. Shooting her in the chest thing.

Selanio:
Like you're sorry.

Stesha:
I was abusing my powers, I shouldn't have done it.

Selanio:
Abusing your… pffft. Like you even hurt her.

Selan:
Hey, it hurt! It just didn't, you know, leave any sort of damage.

Selanio:
This is what I said.

Selan:
Buu.

Stesha:
Look, just accept the apology already.

Selanio (sitting up):

You know, you're not acting like your smarmy self.

Selan:

Hey, yeah. You aren't smiling way too much.

Stesha:

I just got out of my least favorite class, then had to go smile, smile, smile at that damn teacher after class and tell her about how she was a damn inspiration to me and how I'm going to turn things around and work harder just to get her to turn my F into a D. Why the hell do you think I'd be in a mood to pretend to be friendly to people that I know aren't going to fall for it?

Selan:

Good point.

Selanio:

Why are you even bothering apologizing?

Stesha:

Because I don't want you to kill me in my sleep.

Selanio:

I make no promises.

Selan:

You know, generally when you apologize for something, you should be a little more, you know… sincere?

Stesha:

I'm sincere. I *sincerely* don't want my ass kicked by this freakshow.

(Selanio punches Stesha in the face.)

Stesha (on the ground):

I should've seen that coming…

Selan:

Seriously.

Selanio:

Go away, jackass.

Stesha:

Fine.

(He gets up and walks off.)

Selan:
Sheeeesh. What a loser. **(She writes a little more on her notebook.)** Selanio, don't you think this kanji looks like a guy with a big head?

Selanio:
No.

Selan:
I think it looks like a guy with a big head.

Selanio:
I think you're weird. u_u

Selan:
Buu. Anyway, Selan has to get to her social studies class.

Selanio:
Yeah, yeah.

Selan:
You should go home and work on your homework! I know you have some.

Selanio:
I don't want to.

Selan:
Do it. u_u Anyway, see you.

(Selan leaves. Selanio lies there for a moment then, seeing that there's nothing to do, decides that he might as well go home after all. He walks off, but as he's passing between two buildings, he runs into Stesha again.)

Selanio:
Zitomira.

Stesha:
Oi, lemme talk to you for a second.

Selanio:
No.

Stesha:
Why do you bother hanging out with her?

Selanio:
What, Selan?

Stesha:
Yeah.

Selanio:
You should be one to talk, you were the one that kept hitting on her. -_O

Stesha:
I was just scoping her out is all.

Selanio:
Whatever.

Stesha:
Look, she's not like us.

Selanio:
'Us'?

Stesha:
You know what I mean. **(He looks around.)** She doesn't have… powers.

Selanio (suddenly wary):
… I don't either, jackass.

Stesha:
That's a lie and you know it.

Selanio (narrowing his eyes):
What do you want?

Stesha:
What makes you think I want anything? **(He smiles.)** I'm just trying to warn you, Selanio. Selan isn't one of us.

Selanio:
That… that's right, she isn't! So what?

Stesha:
She'll never understand you. It'd never work out, a god like you and a mortal like her.

Selanio:

What makes you think—

Stesha:

You ought to seek out someone like you, someone with powers. Lady Ira, perhaps. Surely you know how to contact her, don't you… *Baron?*

Selanio:

What makes you think Selanio has any interest in either Selan or Ira?!

Stesha:

I wonder. **(He puts his hands in his pockets.)** Oh, and just so you know; I wouldn't dare to reveal your identity to anyone. But if you go telling anyone of my powers… well, I suppose I wouldn't be able to make any promises then, hm?

Selanio:

Pfft. Like anyone would even *care* about your powers.

Stesha:

Right. n_n So don't go opening your mouth.

Selanio:

Fine, whatever! Just get out of my sight.

(Selanio pushes Stesha out of the way and stomps off. Stesha watches him intently as he goes.)

Stesha:

See you around, mate~ n_n

-End: Episode sixty-six.

067. Fair enough.

(The scene is the Agency headquarters. After weeks of trying to figure out who the head of the Agency is and where his office might be, Clovis has resorted to sneaking around. He looks around to make sure no one's around, then pushes a button on his watch, which is apparently a walkie-talkie.)

Clovis:
Okay, so you're sure that this is the boss-man's office?

Osias (on the walkie-talkie):
No, I'm not. All I know is that the map has this room unmarked.

Clovis:
Sheesh… Okay, well… I'll try it, anyway.

Osias:
Are you sure this is necessary? I mean, I don't think the boss wants us poking our noses around…

Clovis:
Don't worry about it, I won't tell them you helped. And they won't do much to me, the government owes me.

Anyway—here I go!

(Clovis throws the door open to find—what looks like a storage room. He sighs, walking in and closing the door behind him. He pushes the button on his watch again.)

Clovis:

There's nothing here. Looks like storage.

Osias:

Odd. We already have a storage room.

Clovis:

Do you think that—

Osias:

No, the other storage room isn't secretly the boss' office. I was in there just yesterday.

Clovis:

Damn.

Osias:

Well, maybe you should get out of there. I mean, that's a secret area, you could get in trouble if anyone finds you.

Clovis:

Don't worry about it. I think I'll just snoop around a bit more.

(Clovis starts moving things around and peeking into boxes. He sees little of interest—papers, computer parts, office supplies and the like. Groaning, he knocks over a stack of boxes and sits on one of the fallen computer monitors, annoyed. He sits there for a few minutes, trying to figure out how he's going to figure things out.)

(Eventually, he hears a noise behind him.)

(He looks back and sees a door. He scratches his head, sure that the door hadn't been there before. He pushes the button on his watch.)

Clovis:

Hey… Adamina.

Osias:

Yeah?

Clovis:

Does that map of yours show another door in here?

Osias:

You mean a door besides the one you entered from?

Clovis:

Yeah.

Osias:

No. Why?

Clovis:

… No reason.

(Clovis gets up and opens the door. There's a hallway behind it. Clovis walks down it to find another door, which he opens. He walks through to find a plain, white-walled office. There's a desk on the other side of the room. Someone sits in a chair, facing away from Clovis. The back of the chair obscures whoever is sitting there.)

Clovis:

Hey look, there's a room here.

(Clovis steps forward, closing the door behind him. He waits to see if the person at the desk will respond, but he doesn't.)

Clovis:

So I'm hoping you're the boss-man, because I've had some nagging questions that I'm dying to ask that guy.

(Still no answer.)

Clovis:

You gonna ignore me?

???:

I am merely waiting for you to begin your questioning.

Clovis:

Ah. Fair enough. … I don't suppose you could turn around so I can see who I'm talking to?

(There is a pause, and then the chair turns around. In the seat sits a pale man with blonde hair and blue eyes. He wears the same clothes and glasses that Indrid does.)

Clovis:
Hah, I should've known. You're some sort of friend of Indrid's.

???:
Indeed. You may call me Smith.

Clovis:
Damn, well that answers one question… obviously if you're Indrid's buddy, that explains how you're able to communicate with him.

Smith:
Of course.

Clovis:
So, what, are you an alien like him? You don't really look like him, besides the creepy look on your face.

Smith:
We are similar, yes.

Clovis (sitting down in the chair across from Smith):
And you're in charge of this Agency?

Smith:
Indeed.

Clovis:
So… do you have the same powers as Indrid?

Smith:
To some extent. My ability to anticipate future events is a bit lacking compared to his, but otherwise our abilities are almost the same.

Clovis:
But that means… not only do you know the identity of every superhero—since you're the boss here—but you must also know the identity of every villain, too!

Smith:
I do.

Clovis:
Shit, man, and you don't *use* that information?

Smith:
There is a balance to the world. It is not my place to interfere.

Clovis:
Then what the hell is all this?!

(He motions at the office.)

Smith:
I merely give your people the means to maintain the balance themselves.

Clovis:
Ugh, *just* like Indrid. **(He pauses, remembering something.)** You know, did it ever occur to him that he didn't have to create a new superhero and villain just to chase off some aliens? He could've called on some *existing* superheroes.

Smith:
Indrid is very discerning.

Clovis:
So he didn't like any of the existing options.

Smith:
Correct.

Clovis:
Jesus.

(There's a silence for a minute, as Clovis thinks about things and Smith just… kinda sits there.)

Clovis:
So… what *is* all this? I mean, with Indrid it's obvious what he's doing, he's protecting the world from like aliens and asteroids and shit. What's your deal?

Smith:
Mister Kuld and I have worked for millennia to protect the Earth. He protects the Earth from harm from external sources, whereas I protect it from threats from within.

Clovis:

So you're trying to keep us from blowing each other up?

Smith:

Something like that, yes.

Clovis:

… by controlling all of the country's superheroes.

Smith:

Not just this country's. I am also the head of every other similar agency all over the world.

Clovis:

Holy hell, man. So why'd you let me find you?

Smith:

Well, first, from your previous history it is clear that you are capable of keeping this a secret…

Clovis:

Right…

Smith:

And also, it is obvious that you would not get any work done until you found the truth.

Clovis:

You could've just come up with some sort of lie.

Smith:

You would not have fallen for it.

Clovis:

No, I suppose not.

Smith:

Now then. I do not suppose you could leave and go back to work, could you? I do believe there is still a mountain of paperwork sitting on your desk.

Clovis:

You can read my mind, why can't *you* just fill out the paperwork for me?

Smith:

Because then I would not have any reason to keep you

on our payroll.

Clovis:

-_- Damn…

Smith:

Go on. I will see you in time.

(Smith turns his chair around again. Clovis scratches his head, then turns and leaves. He walks down the hall, back into the storage room and out into the outer hallway. As he leaves, the door to Smith's office disappears, leaving no evidence that it was ever there at all.)

-End: Episode sixty-seven.

068. I'd sign up for that.

(The scene is a store. Damon and Dorcia are there. Dorcia is just standing around while Damon is looking at… underwear. Soon, Selan, Selanio and Xeno walk by on their way to somewhere else in the store and see them.)

Selan:
Hey, it's the Lordses~

Damon (blushing):
Oh! He-hello.

Selan:
What'cha dooooin'?

Damon:
W-well, I…

Selanio:
He's shopping for underwear, stupid. u_u

Damon:
Yes…

Selan:

Oh. Duh! But that's so mundane! You're this big billionaire CEO guy! Don't you have servants to buy your undapants for you?

Xeno:

What, like a boxers delivery service?

Selan:

Yeah! Man, that'd be awesome. I'd sign up for that.

Damon:

I couldn't ask a servant to buy my underpants for me. It'd be embarrassing…

Selanio:

You're acting embarrassed enough shopping for them yourself.

Dorcia:

He is easily flustered. -_-

Selan:

Seriously. Hey, Dorcia! Why don't you buy his undapants for him? I mean, wives buy their husbands undapants all the time.

Damon:

That is embarrassing too…

Xeno:

Jeezus, man, you're hopeless.

Damon:

I know. -_-;

Dorcia:

Here, just buy these ones and let us be done with this.

Damon:

Okay… 6_6;

Selan:

Hey, you wanna hang out once you buy those?

Damon:

Alright. ^^;;

(Damon and Dorcia go to the cashier to pay for the underpants.)

Selanio:
Why do we want to hang out with them, now?

Selan:
They're cool! Also they're rich and powerful. So shut up and be polite.

Xeno:
Yeah, don't piss off Dorcia. You remember what she did to you that one time. -_O

Selanio:
I was fine in two days!

Selan:
Considering you recover from most injuries in *one* day, I'd say that's pretty bad.

Selanio:
Hmph…

(Damon and Dorcia return.)

Damon:
We're back. ^^;

Selan:
Yaaaay~ Where shall we hang out?

Selanio:
I thought we were on our way to buy me some new bowties…

Selan:
You have enough bowties to last you ten lifetimes. u_u Let's do something actually fun.

Dorcia:
… Coffee.

Xeno:
Huh?

Dorcia:
Let us get some coffee.

Selanio:
Yeah, sure, okay.

(They go to a nearby coffee place. They get their various drinks and sit down at a couch.)

Selan (noting Dorcia's huge, high-caffeine drink):
You know, that caffeine will kill you. u_u

Dorcia:
Silence. -_O

Selanio:
No, I get it! The caffeine is what lets her move so fast!

Selan:
Hey, yeah! I never thought of that!

Dorcia:
-_- Stop being so stupid.

Damon:
She just likes her coffee. n_n That's all there is to it, really.

Selan:
Do you know a guy named Godot…?

Selanio:
No! We agreed on this! No more stupid obscure references!

Selan:
It's not obscure, everyone's played Phoenix Wright!

Damon:
I don't think I have…

Selanio:
There, you see?!

Selan:
Aww, man…

Xeno:
So how go things?

Damon:
As well as can be hoped.

Xeno:
How's your brother doing? He hasn't tried to break out of jail, has he?

Dorcia:
He has. But they have been keeping him in a supervillain jail, so he does not have much hope of escape.

Xeno:
Oh, good.

Damon:
It is a shame that things had to happen this way. -_-; He may have tried to kill me, but he *is* my brother…

Dorcia:
He is a louse. I hope he rots.

Selan:
Uh… changing the subject.

Selanio:
Seriously.

Selan:
How's the marriage? Romantic and lovey, I hope?

Damon:
Oh, of course. n_n We couldn't be happier.

Dorcia:
Yes.

(She drinks some coffee.)

Damon:
We have been considering having children.

Dorcia:
Nothing definite though.

Damon:
Right. ^^;

Selan:
Aw man, tiny corporate CEOs running around!

Selanio:
Adorable. 9_9

Selan:
Do it guys! Make babies! Babies EVERYWHERE.

Dorcia:
… -_O

Selan:
Can you let me babysit? I love kids. =3 … in small quantities. ^_^

Selanio:
Pffft, like these rich people would hire you when they can get fancy high-quality nannies.

Selan:
I'm high-quality =<

Selanio:
Yeah, a high-quality weirdo.

Damon (laughing nervously):
Ahh, you three are so amusing.

Dorcia:
I am not sure if that is the appropriate word.

Xeno:
You can call them freaks, it's okay. -_-;

Damon:
^^; Ahaha…

Dorcia (finishing her coffee):
You have a board meeting in a half hour.

Damon:
Do I? Can't I skip it?

Dorcia:
You skipped the last one. The shareholders were displeased.

Damon:
Agh, you're right…

Selan:
You guys gotta go?

Damon:
Yes. Sorry to leave so soon.

Selanio:
Not a problem at all. u_u

Damon:
Take care of yourselves. n_n Try not to get into too much trouble.

(Damon and Dorcia both leave. Our villains sit there, drinking their drinks for a moment.)

Selanio:
… >_<

Selan:
What?

Selanio:
Now that he said not to, I gotta go cause some trouble. Let's blow up an orphanage.

Xeno:
Maybe not an orphanage… but okay, let's go.

Selan:
Selan never says no to destruction! Yay~

(The three run off to destroy things.)

-End: Episode sixty-eight.

069. New temporary sidekick

(It's a Saturday. Tavvy walks into the Professor's office, having been called there. He enters to see Audi and the Professor in there—Audi's in what looks like a makeshift superhero costume. The Professor looks… displeased.)

Tavvy:
Uh… what's going on?

Audi:
My birthday's coming up!

Tavvy:
Uhhkay…

Audi:
I asked daddy to let me be your sidekick for the day instead of giving me a proper present. ^_^

Marika:
She can't ask for an iPod, or a new cell phone or something like other girls, no…

Audi:
This is much better! And besides, I can ask for that

iPod next Christmas.

Marika:
Ugh…

Tavvy:
And no one asked *me* if this was okay…?

Marika:
Oh, of course not.

Audi:
It's only for one day! And besides, you've always wanted a sidekick, right?

Tavvy:
Uh… I guess. What if nothing happens today?

Audi:
Well then I guess I'll be your sidekick for two days.

Tavvy:
Okay…

Marika:
Have you even thought of a name for yourself?

Audi:
Er… ^^;;

Tavvy:
… the TA of Terror?

Audi:
What?

Tavvy:
Well if your dad's Professor Pain… ^^;

Marika:
Tavarius, please refrain from being such a loser. -_-;

Tavvy:
Hey!

Marika:
Apsis should be appropriate.

Audi:

Apsis?

Marika:

Look it up.

Tavvy:

Wikipedia, awaaaay~

(Tavvy's watch goes off.)

Marika:

I suppose you can look it up later, then...

Audi:

Yay! Who is it?

Tavvy:

It's Ira's group. Let's go.

(They leave. The Professor sits down, sighing.)

Marika:

Why couldn't she be one of those girls who just likes to be normal...

(Not long after, Apogee and Apsis arrive on the scene to find Ira's group trying to run off with a huge sack of money—not to mention loads of jewelry they've piled onto themselves.)

Apogee:

Stop right there!

Lady Ira:

Uwaaaa~ Such a lame line~

Omen:

Hey, who's the girl?

Apsis:

I'm Apogee's new temporary sidekick, Apsis!

Baron von Boom:

"Temporary"? Lame. u_u

Lady Ira:

Apsis? Ohhh, I get it! Apogee, Apsis... clever! You know a lot of Astronomy stuff, Apogee?

Apogee:

No, the Professor came up with both of our names…

Apsis (a little thrown off by the harmless banter):

A-anyway! We're not gonna let you get away with your evil misdeeds, villains!

Lady Ira:

Even lamer line~ Buu. -_-; **(She adjusts the stolen crown she's wearing.)** King Ira will punish you for being so lame!

Apsis:

… King Ira? But you're a girl…

Lady Ira:

But male titles sound so much more powerful! "Queen" just makes me sound like I'm the doting wife of some fat king.

Apogee:

There've been powerful queens in history.

Lady Ira:

But not nearly as many as there were powerful kings! It's sexism, really, calling the ladies by a different name just to keep them down… So I'm *King* Ira. u_u So there.

Apogee:

… uh…

Lady Ira:

Or maybe Emperor Ira? Ooh, ooh, or PHAROH Ira!

Apogee:

… right then. Well, King or Queen, we're gonna kick your butts. u_u

Apsis:

Yeah! You tell 'em!

Baron von Boom:

Enough of this little loser-party.

(He starts shooting energy bolts at the superheroes. Apogee dodges out of the way, and Apsis covers her face, taking the hit with little effect.)

Omen:

Hm. She actually has superpowers, then.

Lady Ira:

Not bad.

Apsis:

Yeah, I'm really superpowered! You guys don't stand a chance!

Lady Ira:

Sure. u_u … Omen, hold her.

Omen:

Sure thing.

(Omen grabs a nearby stop sign and hits Apsis with it, then proceeds to wrap it around her.)

Lady Ira:

Arrite, Baron, take things from here!

Apogee:

Hey, no fair! Don't pick on her, she's still a rookie!

Lady Ira:

No man, it's cool, it's like an initiation. We gotta do it! She can't be a real hero unless we do!

Apogee:

The Professor will kill me if anything happens to her!

Baron von Boom:

Not our problem. u_u

(The Baron runs over and winds up to punch Apsis, but she breaks out of the stop sign and dodges, punching the Baron in the side as she does so.)

Baron von Boom:

You pack a hell of a punch for such a tiny girl >_O But not enough of a punch, I'm afraid. u_u

(He continues to fight with her—she dodges awkwardly, obviously not experienced with fighting and not really sure what to do.)

Apsis:

You know, **(She manages to land a punch, but not a very good one.)** I always thought it was weird you were a villain. You're way too pretty to be evil, really!

Baron von Boom:

Well, I *am* pretty. u_u A face like this should rule the world!

Apsis:

=< Buu, the pretty ones always have to be bad. **(She punches him again.)**

Omen:

How come I never get 'you're too pretty to be evil' talks? -_-;

Lady Ira:

Seriously! Why not me? =<

Apogee:

Because you're all losers. u_u

(Apogee lunges at Omen and Ira, but Ira blocks. Baron von Boom knocks Apsis over and proceeds to throw her at Apogee.)

Lady Ira:

Omen, quick, pile some stuff on them so we can run.

(Omen nods, then lifts a few cars and tosses them into a pile on top of the heroes. Ira then throws a smoke bomb–style, remember!–and the three run off, money, jewels and all.)

Apogee:

Ugh… ouch…

Apsis:

… sniffle…

Apogee (pushing the cars off):

Are you okay?

Apsis (starting to cry):

Yeah…

Apogee (not really sure what to do):

A-are you sure? What's wrong?

Apsis:
I let the bad guys get away…

Apogee:
Hey, it's okay, I mean, you were stuck under a car…

Apsis:
You totally could've taken them on your own… I ruined everything.

Apogee:
Hey, hey… it's your first time doing this, fighting crime is hard!

Apsis:
You didn't lose like this your first time.

Apogee:
I'd been training for months at that point. You haven't. It's okay, no one'll hold it against you.

Apsis:
But… what about all that money and…?

Apogee:
That bank was insured, it's okay. They'll get their money back.

Apsis:
Really?

Apogee:
Yeah. Don't worry about it. But uh… your dad's probably gonna use this against you next time you ask to do the heroing thing… ^^;;

Apsis:
Aw, jeez… ;o;

-End: Episode sixty-nine.

Apsis:
Why did the bank have crowns in it anyway?

Apogee:
Don't ask me, man, no one tells me anything.

070. Some revolution!

(Our villains are watching TV while eating chips. The show they were watching has just ended, and the news starts.)

Selanio:
Where's the remote?

Selan:
Hey we can't flip it yet! We gotta watch the news!

Selanio:
That's boring.

Selan:
It's important that we know what's going on in town! That way we know what banks to rob, whether there's any roads we shouldn't take when running away, that sort of thing.

Xeno:
She's right. Foresight, man.

Selanio:
You can look that up online. C'mon, let's watch House or something.

Selan:
It's a rerun anyway! Spoiler: IT'S NOT LUPUS.

Xeno (actually watching the news):
Hey, Quantum's on.

Selan:
Hm? Ooh, live footage! What's he doing, robbing someplace?

Selanio:
Looks like he's blowing stuff up.

Selan:
Also good! Go, Bria—ehh? What just—

(On the TV, Brian has been shot out of the sky by… something.)

Selan:
Guys was that…?

Xeno:
That didn't look like Apogee's lasers. It looked more like…

(Reza appears on screen—first as a dot atop a building, but then the cameraman notices him and zooms in.)

Selan (jumping to her feet):
Shit! Costume up, guys!!

(Selan runs to her room. The others look bewildered.)

Xeno:
You want to go help him?

Selan (from her room):
We have to! Reza hates normal people, remember? If he's acknowledging Brian at all it's because he wants to do something horrible to him! **(She runs back in, in costume.)** Brian's our homie. We gotta protect him!

Selanio:
He's not our homie, he's more like an annoying neighbor.

Xeno:

Apogee can handle this, I'm sure he'll be fine.

Lady Ira:

I don't trust Apogee for a second to protect Brian. We gotta stick up for our allies, guys! Get changed now, King Ira demands it!

Xeno (shrugging):

Well, if you're sure…

(He goes to his room.)

Selanio:

If we get killed it's all your fault. -_-;

(Selanio goes to get changed too.)

(Not long after, it's the downtown area and Quantum is hiding behind a billboard atop a building, trying to catch his breath. Meanwhile Apogee has finally showed up and is arguing with Reza.)

Reza:

He's a criminal anyway, isn't he? Don't get in my way!

Apogee:

Just because he's a crook doesn't mean I can let you kill him! It's kind of against the law!

(Quantum relaxes, glad that Apogee's providing a decent enough distraction. His phone goes off—luckily it's on vibrate, so it doesn't make enough noise to give away his position. He answers it.)

Quantum (whispering):

Not a good time…

Ann (phone):

Are you okay?! I saw you get hit!

Quantum (still whispering):

I'm a little hurt, but mostly okay. I'll be back as soon as I can get out of here.

Ann (phone):

Okay. Good luck.

Quantum (whispering again):

Thanks. Bye.

(He hangs up. He starts looking around to see if there's any route he can take that wouldn't be visible to Reza. He turns to the side—to find Ira all up in his face. He falls over, surprised.)

Quantum (trying to yell quietly??):

Wh-what the fuck? Don't sneak up on me like that!

Lady Ira:

That's a fine hello =< We're here to save you and you yell at us!

Baron von Boom:

See, he's being a loser, let's just go. u_u

Quantum:

Shh! You're going to attract his attention.

Lady Ira:

Right right, sorry. Look, let's get you out of here okay?

Quantum:

I can escape by myself.

Omen:

Don't be stubborn. -_-; If he spots you he'll kill you. At least Ira can protect you.

Lady Ira:

Yeah. So let's go before—

(Just then, Apogee comes crashing through the billboard. He skids along the rooftop, groaning. He looks around, seeing Quantum and Ira's group.)

Apogee:

Shit…

(Reza jumps over, chasing Apogee, but quickly notices the others. He ignores Ira's group and promptly tries to blast the hell out of Quantum, but Ira jumps in front of him and covers him in a barrier. The blast dissipates on contact.)

Reza:

What do you think you're doing?

Lady Ira (Still holding up the barrier):

Seriously man, what's it look like?

Reza:

Get out of my way.

Lady Ira:

Sorry, no can do.

Reza:

What's wrong with you? First this one **(he points at Apogee)** won't let me attack this human, and now you? Is he not your competition?

Lady Ira:

He's not our competition, he's our buddy. =<

Reza:

So you would ally yourself with him, but not with me?

Lady Ira:

Yup!

Omen:

Please note that you were asking for our *obedience*, whereas with Quantum we just kind of like to hang out sometimes. It's something else entirely.

Baron von Boom:

Seriously, mister big sensitive baby. -_O

Reza:

Grr…

Apogee:

Not to break anything up, but—

(Reza blasts Apogee, knocking him back a little ways.)

Reza:

This doesn't concern you!!

Lady Ira:

Look, Reza, I know you're trying to, like, destroy normal people and stuff, but seriously Quantum's cool. Why are you picking on him?

Reza:
He dares try to stand against a superpowered hero. He must pay for his hubris.

Apogee (brushing dust out of his hair):
Uh… and you stand against me too, I'm not sure I understand your logic…

Baron von Boom:
It's crazy person logic, the best thing to do is just say "you're stupid" and hope they go away. -_-;

Reza:
>_< Silence, all of you!

Lady Ira:
Look, Reza, let's be reasonable. You think superpowered people should be in charge, right? Fine. *I'm* in charge here. This is my city, my territory. Follow?

Apogee:
I'm not sure that—

Omen:
Shut it. >_O

Lady Ira:
And I, *King Ira*, get to choose whether or not Quantum gets to hang around these parts, and I say he's cool.

Baron von Boom (under his breath):
Ugh, how long is she going to keep calling herself "King"…?

Reza:
… I do not recognize your authority.

Lady Ira:
Don't be a stubborn prick. You're only saying that because I'm disagreeing with you. If I said "This is my territory and you CAN vaporize my friend", you'd be all like "Oh Ira your authority is AWESOME."

(Reza's had enough of this. He charges energy into his hand and punches Ira's barrier. It fails to break through, but he keeps at it. Ira flinches—while her barrier's okay, he's

definitely making it hard to keep her barrier up. The Baron notices Ira's difficulty and steps in, blasting at Reza. Reza jumps away, returning fire. Baron von Boom gets knocked over, but he gets back up right away.)

Baron von Boom:

Lame-ass! You aren't welcome here, Reza, this is our town! Don't you realize why no one wants to join you? It's because you're fucking nuts and you pull shit like this!

Apogee:

Seriously! Some revolution! You're not going to make a bit of difference if all you ever manage to do is piss people off.

Reza:

Grr…!!

(Reza rushes forward, ready to tear them all a new one, when suddenly he finds a chunk of broken billboard lodged in his stomach. He stops, shocked.)

Omen (who just threw the piece of billboard):

Thank you, thank you, I'm here all week. u_u

Reza:

You…! You'll… you'll pay for this!!

Omen:

Try it. Anytime.

Baron von Boom:

Hah! Go Omen!

(Reza is enveloped by energy and he teleports away. The Baron slaps Omen on the back.)

Baron von Boom:

Aw man, that was sneaky! I didn't know you had it in you!

Omen:

Someone had to get him to go away.

Lady Ira (paying more attention to Quantum):

You okay, man? It looked like you got hit pretty hard on the TV.

Quantum:

I'm fine, jeez. What's your problem? Don't you realize that Reza's going to be out for your blood now?

Lady Ira:

I know. But I couldn't let you get vaporized. I'd never be able to face Chandra. =<

Quantum:

-_-; Thanks, I guess. But I didn't need your help.

Apogee:

Yeah you did. If she hadn't been there when Reza found you you would've been a dead man.

Quantum:

Shut the fuck up, you. >_O

Lady Ira:

Yeah, loser! … although the loser is right. -_-;

Apogee:

Will you guys be alright? Reza's really dangerous, and he looked pretty pissed at you.

Baron von Boom:

Pffft. If you can hold your own against him, then surely WE can. u_u

Apogee:

Well… just know that if you fight against him, then I'll fight him with you.

Lady Ira:

… and NOW I feel lousy about this decision. ><

Apogee:

What? What's wrong with fighting with me?

Lady Ira:

You're a loser!

Apogee:

9_9 Whatever. But we've got a common enemy here so I don't think you should hesitate to work with me if you have to. Anyway, I'm getting out of here. I won't try to arrest you guys right now, all things considered.

(Apogee flies away.)

Quantum (looking away):
… thanks again. I—I should probably get going, before Ann worries too much.

Lady Ira:
Try to lay low for a while, okay? Until this Reza stuff blows over.

Quantum (grinning):
Just until I make something that'll put him in his place.

Omen:
Love the attitude, but you should seriously just avoid villaining for a while.

Quantum:
Pff. See you around.

(Quantum flies off. The three stand there for a moment.)

Lady Ira:
… well!

Baron von Boom:
Well…

Omen:
We're dead men.

Lady Ira:
Absolutely. -_-;

Baron von Boom:
That guy was going to add us to his kill list eventually.

Omen:
That's probably true.

Lady Ira:
I guess we'll just have to hope we can handle this.

Baron von Boom:
And hope he doesn't blow my cover.

Lady Ira:

… and that. Yes.

Omen:

Goddamn…

Lady Ira:

-_-; Let's just go home.

Omen:

Right then.

-End: Episode seventy.

Character Bios

Xenophon Reden

Alias: Omen
Powers: Telekinesis, limited clairvoyance and telepathy

Xeno didn't join the villaining game by choice, and he's not as motivated as his peers, but he's good at what he does nonetheless.

He's quiet and stoic. He's very interested in the paranormal. He has a problem with overthinking things.

He's still working on his evil laugh.

Selan Hagues

Alias: Lady Ira
Powers: Barrier generation

Selan's a huge weeb, a comic book nerd, and has dreamed of being a supervillain since she was little.

Her powerset is the least impressive out of her team, but she puts it to good use protecting the others. Especially Selanio.

She can be a little out there, but she's an expert at keeping her team together.

Selanio Mikhailovich Roselaniy

Alias: Baron von Boom
Powers: Super strength, energy bolts, super durability, limited healing factor

Selanio is from a long line of Russian supervillains, and his greatest goal is to live up to his father's legacy.

He's brash and really rough around the edges. People assume he's stupid, but he isn't--he just talks before he thinks.

Tavarius Imogene

Alias: Apogee
Powers: Super strength, laser eye beams, limited invulnerability

Apogee's been on the scene about as long as our villains have, but he's still considered to be a rookie hero. He's training under Professor Marika, the world's best hero, which are some big shoes to fill.

He's shy and easily embarrassed, but he can fake confidence well enough when he's in costume.

Brian Pazzesco

Alias: Quantum
Powers: Super science

Brian's a lot like most kids his age: he's angry and he has a lot to prove. Unlike most kids his age, he can build a mean laser cannon.

He overdoes things sometimes, which is why it's such a good thing that he has Ann around to keep him in check.

Ann Amor

Alias: Chandra
Powers: Super science

Ann isn't very evil, but she likes to do what Brian does, and Brian's pretty determined to do the villainy thing.

It gives her an excuse to build cool things, so she doesn't mind.

She might just be the greatest scientific mind of the century, but she's too young to be taken seriously yet.

Cathal Fordon

Alias: Agent 03
Powers: Electrokinesis

Cath is Tavvy's best friend, although it took him an embarrassingly long time to figure out that his friend is a superhero.

He has a skewed moral compass. He doesn't go out of his way to do bad things, but he'll do them anyway if it benefits him. Despite that, he'll do anything to defend people he cares about.

Clovis Harlan

Alias: ~~Agent 02~~
Powers: Gravity manipulation

Clovis is a very no-nonsense kind of person. He might be one of the more powerful supers out there, but it's hard to get him to give enough of a fuck to try that hard.

He doesn't pretend to be a good person, but he has drawn lines in the sand that he doesn't like to cross.

He dresses well and smokes too much.

Dorcia Kamaria

Alias: Agent 01
Powers: Super speed, can create energy weapons

Dorcia doesn't talk much. She grew up with Damon and Dalix, and is particularly close to Damon. After finding out that he wasn't dead, she decided to put a ring on it.

Damon Lords

Alias: None
Powers: Mind control

Damon is the head of the Lords corporation, which mostly produces pharmaceuticals. His brother Dalix tried to have him killed to try to take over the business.

He's kind of shy, and tries to avoid conflict. He especially avoids using his powers, for moral reasons.

Dalix Lords

Alias: None
Powers: Super durability, fear control

Dalix didn't inherit the family business, and he's mad about it.

Unfortunately for him, he's stuck in jail now. He seems to have hired Annick Zitomira as the new lawyer for the Lords corporation before he was arrested, though...

Prof. Pavel Marika

Alias: Professor Pain
Powers: Super strength, super speed, invulnerability

The Professor was one of the world's most famous heroes when he retired. He still seems to be at the top of his game, despite his reluctance to use his powers.

He's very stern, and he's known for being the scariest teacher on campus.

Prof. Aldon Sezja

Alias: None
Powers: Super science

Aldon's basically the good guy version of a mad scientist. He works for the Heroes Agency and builds things for them.

Mostly jetpacks.

He looks like he's 12, but he's actually in his fifties. Don't ask.

Indrid Kuld

Alias: Too many to list
Powers: Complete understanding of causality

Indrid is an alien intelligence that has watched over humanity for millenia.

He taught Xeno how to use his powers and he lives on the moon.

Considering the power he has at his fingertips, it's a little weird that he's such a slob.

Smith Smith

Alias: None
Powers: Slightly less complete understanding of causality

Smith is an alien intelligence that has watched over humanity for a little less time than Indrid has.

He runs the Heroes Agency, as well as every equivalent agency around the globe.

Tynan Fordon

Alias: Ohm
Powers: Electrokinesis

Tynan is Cathal's more-talented older cousin. He's a superhero who patrols the Washington, DC area.

He's a little full of himself, but he's got the skills to back it up.

Osias Adamina

Alias: None
Powers: Owns a gun

Osias works for the Heroes Agency and is friends with Clovis. Normally he does paperwork, and he doesn't have superpowers, but he's not completely useless in a fight.

Quentin Dace

Alias: Shockwave
Powers: Creates shockwaves

Quentin is a veteran superhero who used to work with the Professor back in the day.

He's very serious, and isn't good at small talk.

Joseph Pazzesco

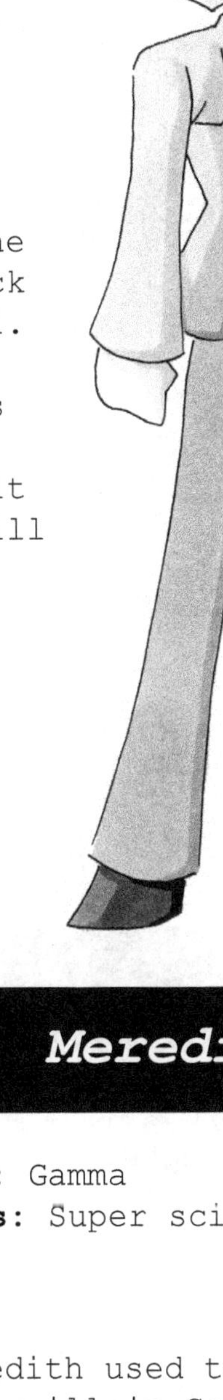

Alias: Beta
Powers: None

Joseph was once the supervillain Beta, before he was arrested. Now he's stuck in a prison mental hospital.

He believes that if he acts cheerful enough, he'll actually be happy. So far it hasn't worked, but he's still trying!

Meredith Pazzesco

Alias: Gamma
Powers: Super science

Meredith used to be the supervillain Gamma, before she became a mom and gave that life up.

She also never tried to break her husband out of jail, but her reasons are unknown.

Dannielle Miniver

Alias: None
Powers: Psychic, but only on vending machines.

Danni is a computer science major at the university, and thinks Tavvy is super cute.

She's observant, has a million and one tech support stories, and always has a ton of homework.

Audi Marika

Alias: Apsis (temporarily)
Powers: Super strength, invulnerability.

Audi is the Professor's daughter. She's very knowledgeable about heroes and villains, despite the fact that her dad tries to keep her out of that life.

She has the potential to grow as strong as the Professor, but whether he'd ever let her become a hero is another story altogether.

Stesha Zitomira

Alias: None
Powers: Useless eye laser

Stesha and Selanio used to be friends in high school, but that friendship soured into an intense rivalry. It isn't clear what Stesha did to make Selanio hate him, but he's slimy enough that it must have been pretty bad.

He has a bad habit of picking fights he can't win.

Annick Zitomira

Alias: Reza
Powers: Spooky black energy

Reza was a villain back in the Professor's day, and he was the most dangerous villain there was.

Now he's back, and he's ready to finish what he started all those years ago.

CPSIA information can be obtained
at www.ICGtesting.com
Printed in the USA
LVHW101811250419
615550LV00007B/210/P

9 781974 145188